Silas Erie Paranormal Cozy #1

GHOST
IN THE
CUPBOARD

Chase Connor

Book Cover Designed By:
©2026 Chase Connor; Chase Connor Books

Published By:

Chase Connor Books
www.chaseconnor.com

E-book ISBN 978-1-951860-55-4
Paperback ISBN 978-1-951860-56-1

Between Enzo & the Universe
(narrated by Brian Lore Evans; Tantor Media)
Head for Murder – Head Rock Harbor Mystery #1
(narrated by Nick Trengove)
Murder in the Rough – Head Rock Harbor Mystery #2
(narrated by Nick Trengove)
Pride and Puncture – Head Rock Harbor Mystery #3
(narrated by Nick Trengove)
Bang Bang He Shot Her Down – Head Rock Harbor Mystery #4
(narrated by Nick Trengove)

<u>Translated</u>

Between Enzo & the Universe – **Spanish**
A Surplus of Light – **Spanish**

CHAPTER 1

Dear Mr. Silas Eerie,

Thank you for applying for the Waterson Altruism Grant. Waterson Corporations is pleased to be in a position to extend assistance to organizations helping those in need in our communities through our grant program. Thousands of applications are received yearly, and this year was no exception. While we find your cause to be worthy of one of our prestigious grants, we regret to inform you that—

Crumbling up the single sheet of white printer paper, I didn't bother to read the rest of the letter. A rejection is a rejection whether you read the entire thing or not. Besides, I'd known that my application was denied the moment I saw the way my last name had been spelled in the greeting. If someone can't be bothered to get the spelling of your name correct, you're obviously of no importance to them. Hence, you are not worthy of one of the grants they bestow upon charitable organizations yearly, and the matter is closed.

Though I wanted to believe that The Lunch Counter simply couldn't compete against other charitable organizations for a Waterson Altruism Grant, I knew the truth. The misspelling of my name wasn't simply an oversight or the mistype of a harried office assistant. The folks at Waterson Corporations had known all about me and The Lunch Counter already. We're common knowledge to anyone in the Midwest. Or anyone who stays up late, doom-scrolling on social media, and finds themselves in a YouTube black hole.

This marked the third year—and third rejection—from the Waterson Corporation for one of their grants. Two rejections in the first two years of applying might have been easily written off as a poorly written grant application. Or maybe the Waterson Corporation waiting to see how dedicated I was before giving me, and The Lunch Counter, a grant. However, with this third rejection—*and the obviously intentional misspelling of my name*—I knew continuing to apply for the grant was a waste of time going forward.

Sighing, I tossed the ball of paper in the bathroom waste basket and returned my attention to the mirror. Grinning like an insane clown, I checked my teeth and gums. I'd flossed, brushed, and rinsed with mouthwash. Sparkling and not a speck of leftover food. I was going to ruin that. I tilted my head back and checked both nostrils. No wild hairs. Titling my head down to look at my brows, I found nothing wild in need of my attention there, either.

Twisting my face back and forth, I reached up and rubbed at my neck, cheeks, chin, and upper lip. I was never great at growing facial hair, but a shave was needed from time to time. Tonight was not going to be one of those times. So, I washed my face and used witch hazel after drying my skin gently with a terry cloth towel. Every day magic is found in rituals. Routines. Having a nightly routine before sliding into bed helps one settle mentally and prepare for slumber.

That's what I tell myself.

Sleep would come whether I went through my routine or not, but settling my mind beforehand simply makes my sleep more restful. Rinsing away the grit of the day helps the body transition from one state to another. A bedtime routine is like the Last Rites at a hospital bed…except you usually wake up the following morning.

After I'd made sure my hygiene and grooming were taken care of, I gave the waste basket a final glance. The ball of crumpled white paper mocked me, but I wasn't going to let it bring me down. I shook my head clear of bad thoughts and forced a smile to my face as I slapped off the lights. A positive attitude and a smile can change anything.

Fake it 'til you make it.

Out of the en suite and back in my bedroom, I turned down the covers on my bed. It was early autumn, so it was a cool, crisp evening. Still not cold enough to bust out the winter blankets, but not warm enough to sleep with merely a sheet and light blanket as I did during summer. I fluffed my pillow and checked to make sure my phone was plugged in and charging on the bedside table. Then I made sure my alarm was set accurately.

After that part of my routine, I checked the windows on the other side of the bed. Both latched. I touched all four corners of the wood trim around each, checking for the cold silver discs. Satisfied with my findings, I left my bedroom and checked the windows in the guest room.

Next was the kitchen and backdoor, then the living room windows and front door. I checked the tiny little window in the hall bathroom and even looked up and checked for the silver discs at all four corners of the panel where the pulldown ladder for the attic is located. Lastly, I went to the end of the hall and checked the lock and corners on the door that led into the atrium—my workroom.

Everything checked out.

Sighing with relief, the anxiety that I hadn't realized I was holding in my joints released its grip on me. I rolled my shoulders and took a few deep breaths. The house was secure for the night. A good night's rest was ahead of me.

Having done my necessary nightly checks, I headed back to the kitchen and popped open the fridge. I leaned my hip against the edge of the fridge door as I stared in at its contents. Eventually, I'd have to get to the grocery store. I'd been putting off a shopping trip for over a week, and the fridge before me was slim pickings.

Refusing to be disappointed, I bent down and grabbed the storage container that held cubed watermelon. I set it on the kitchen table before pulling up my pajama bottoms and retying the drawstring. Recently having lost a few pounds—and not having much booty to begin with—my pants were making the loss known.

Considering the action I'd just committed with my pants, I reopened the fridge and grabbed the container that held cubes of different cheeses. After setting the cheese next to the watermelon, I rummaged in the pantry and extracted one of the few remaining bags of extra buttery microwave popcorn. It was quickly unfolded and popped in the microwave.

Four minutes later, I was propped up in my easy chair, my feet crossed on the ottoman, surrounded by my snacks. Though the brown leather Chesterfield chair and ottoman had seen better days, the wear and tear had been done lovingly. One leg was a little wobbly and the leather needed a good cleaning and conditioning—and there was probably years'-worth of lost pocket change in the crevices—but I loved the set dearly.

Like most of the items in my home, the chair and ottoman had come to me lightly used. Not in perfect condition—yet perfect for my needs—lightly used items that cost little or nothing are my favorite kind of items. Furniture with a history, and pieces that were obviously loved by their previous owners, simply feel more comfortable and integrate into different spaces easily.

You just have to be careful from whom you choose to accept used items. No one wants surprises. Like bed bugs.

Or worse.

My nightly hour-long sci-fi dramedy went by in a flash, as did the snacks I'd prepared for myself. The watermelon container was empty, only kernels of popcorn were left, and the cheese was all but obliterated. As the credits rolled, I patted my belly, wondering if I didn't need to finish the evening strong with something sweet. However, it was announced that a program about unsolved murders was about to begin, right before Victor Grimm's advertisement started, and I rushed to flip the T.V. off with the remote.

The picture on the screen evaporated, as my appetite had, when the ad began.

Shaking my head to clear my thoughts of murders and missing people and fame-chasers, I gathered up my items and exited the living room, using my elbow to get the light switch on the way. I cleaned up in the kitchen quickly and washed my dishes, deciding to leave them in the drain tray for the night. A few water spots never killed anyone.

Impulsively, I checked the kitchen windows, the living room windows, and the front door. Turning the lights off on my way to my room, I couldn't help but check the guest bedroom and the hallway bathroom again. Since I was on a roll, I checked the attic access and the door to the workroom once more. Everything was locked and all the silver was in place.

Standing before the workroom door, I went over the schedule on the white board hung at eye level to the left of it.

With my favorite purple dry erase marker, I'd written out the schedule I'd made for myself for the week. If I didn't keep myself on track, work easily got away from me. Having something to remind me where I needed to be and when ensured that life ran as smoothly as possible.

Chewing at my lip, I mentally calculated how much money all the upcoming clients on the schedule contributed to the budget. If I kept up the same pace for the rest of the month, neither my personal budget, nor that of The Lunch Counter, would suffer any. Of course, if I made more time for in-person clients—the ones that *really* brought in the cash, things would be easier, money-wise. Of course, that would mean more travel, as many clients didn't want to come to Sage Grove.

So many of my online clients wanted an in-person appointment, but they simply couldn't—or wouldn't—come to me. Most of them didn't want to wait until I did a tour, either. If I committed to more travel, I could take more clients. However, that would mean reorganizing my entire personal life and the system we had worked out at The Lunch Counter.

Knowing there was no way I was going to solve my problem before bedtime, I gave up. Tomorrow was a brand-new day and things always seemed to find a way to work. Keeping a positive attitude and a willingness to do what needed to be done, eventually I'd figure something out.

Relieved, I returned to my room, shutting the door behind me and locking it. I turned and checked all four corners. Silver. Silver. Silver. And silver. Subconsciously, I ran a finger over the painted wall next to the door. The green paint felt gritty under my flesh—as would all the walls, ceilings, and floors in the house if I felt of them.

I flipped the light switch, leaving the room cast in the soft golden glow of the bedside lamp. Intending to get into bed, I couldn't help myself. My feet led me directly over to the windows first. I checked all of the corners and all the locks. Everything was secure and the silver was in place. Sighing with relief once more, I started to turn back to my bed.

As I turned, movement in the yard beyond caught my eye. Turning back to the windows, I stared out at the yard, but mostly saw my reflection staring back at me. I reached over and pulled the cord on the bedside lamp, and the reflections from the room disappeared from the window glass.

Outside, under the moonless black sky, the yard was nothing more than dark shapes. The trees surrounding the property were skeletal hands reaching up out of the earth. The bushes under the window shimmied in the brisk autumn breeze, the rustling a symphony. I was convincing myself that I had simply been mistaken when my eyes landed on the thing that had caught my eye.

The figure stepped out of the tree line twenty feet beyond the windows, and into the yard. He was staring down at his feet, walking across the yard towards the house. Dressed in out-of-style worn jeans, brown leather shoes too big for his feet, and a sweater that had likely been knitted for him by an older relative, his shaggy mop of hair hung like vines around his face.

Halfway across the yard to the house, he stopped in his tracks, lifted his head, and looked directly at the window. Our eyes connected, but I could barely see his in the darkness and through the tangles of hair that hung from his head. He grinned widely as he stared across the yard at me.

Black viscous slime oozed from his gums, over his teeth, and down his chin, dripping to the yard below.

INTERLUDE

Or...

What they don't teadch you in school about ghosts.

HAUNTS – Ghosts of those who died naturally. They stick around the place where they died, tied to the spot. They may or may not be vocal and/or retain memories from life. Generally harmless, absolutely annoying.

TICKS – Like "HAUNTS" but attached to a person instead of a place. Will follow those responsible for their death. Feed off of the guilt and grief they make their victims feel. Probably ran an MLM or a religious cult in their human life.

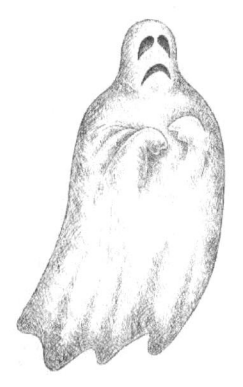

SCREAMERS – These ghosts may or may not travel. May be tied to a place or person. However, they are never talkative or retain memories. They moan, wail, cry, and scream incessantly for attention. Were probably theater kids in their human lives.

TRAVELERS - Ghosts that can travel, searching out their unfinished business. Probably the most vocal and retain the most memories from life. Don't ask their life story. They'll tell you.

HORRORS - Can be Haunts or Ticks, feeding off the fear of those they try to scare. Can become a poltergeist if given too much attention. Or not enough attention. Very emotional. All of them were Cancer zodiac signs in their human lives.

SAPS - May or may not be Travelers. Always feeding off the energy of those who enter their favorite haunting spaces. Love hotels, vacation rentals, and airport lounges. Were likely lifestyle coaches in their humans lives.

BACK TO OUR REGULARLY SCHEDULED PROGRAM...

Without hesitation, I unlatched the window and slid it up so that I could lean out.

"You're oozing again, Chester," I said loudly enough to be heard across the yard. "From the mouth this time."

11

Chester Erie, my great-great-great-something-or-other, shut his mouth, slapping a hand over it in a gentlemanly fashion. His ethereal voice, muffled by his hand, drifted across the yard.

"*Fawry.*"

"It's not bothering me any," I said, reassuring him. "Don't worry about it. Just thought you'd want to know."

Chester stared at me, his mouth covered by his diaphanous hand for a moment longer, then he lowered his arm. His mouth, exposed once again, was clear of the black slime that had been oozing from it seconds previously. That's one of the worst things about ghosts—sometimes they simply can't control their bodies.

Non-bodies?

Shapes?

Vehicles?

Well, whatever it is that a ghost resides in—that is a translucent replica of the body they had in life—can be unpredictable after death. Sometimes it oozes. A piece can fall off and have to be reattached. It's not uncommon for a ghost to not appear at all, only making their presence known through noises and cold drafts.

Ever walk through your house, suddenly get a chill, and wonder what that was all about? Might've been a malfunctioning ghost. You'll never know for certain, because ninety-nine-point-nine percent of the human population can't see them. Which means people like me—what most people would refer to as a "medium"—are considered freaks.

It's hurtful, but I've had nearly thirty years to get over it.

You get called a freak for that long and it begins to feel like a cherished nickname. Or, at least, that's what you learn to start telling yourself.

"Waterson turned us down," I said, leaning on the window sill with my forearms. "Third year running."

Chester frowned deeply.

"*Sapheads*," Chester said. "*The lot of 'em.*"

"Yep." I sighed. "Bunch of butt faces."

He nodded affirmatively and his translucent head wobbled on his neck so precariously that I was afraid it'd roll off into the yard. Over time, I've learned that a lost head for a ghost is not the tragedy it would be for a human being. I've learned to not gasp at the sight of a body part barely hanging on by a thread to the rest of a ghost's body.

"*What will you do now?*" Chester asked, his voice like a moan.

The ghost flickered out of sight for a moment, then appeared once more, like a shoddy lightbulb.

I shrugged.

"What I always do, I guess," I said. "Keep taking as many clients as possible. The Lunch Counter will survive. One way or another."

Chester said nothing, but his eyes seemed to glimmer in the moonlight. At first, I thought he was touched by the sentiment that I would keep The Lunch Counter open at all costs. However, black slime started to drip from the corner of his eyes, and I realized my assessment had been wrong. He was merely malfunctioning.

I've been able to see ghosts for as long as I have memories of being alive. Yet there are still more mysteries about their existence that I haven't solved than those I have. Mysteries that even the ghosts cannot provide answers for—if they're able to speak coherently, that is. Some ghosts can't even get one word out without moaning and rattling chains like a lunatic.

"Well," I said, not bothering to mention the reappearance of the slime, "I'm going to head to bed. Are you on yard duty?"

Chester grinned. His gums were filled with the slime once more. I didn't acknowledge it.

"*I shall alert you immediately of any danger!*" Chester proclaimed proudly.

"Thanks, Chester," I said. "Goodnight."

Chester's head wobbled precariously once more as he nodded to me. Smiling, I stood and pushed the window back down, slapping the lock into place once it was closed. Out of habit, I touched my finger to the silver pieces at each corner of the window, then slid the drapes shut. I tiptoed over to my bed—the same one three generations of Eries had slept in— and further pulled back the covers. Thankfully, it was the frame that had survived for so long and not the mattress. It had been replaced many times over.

Sliding into bed, I sighed as my feet went under the covers, immediately warming up. Even though it was early autumn, the bare floorboards of the house could quickly chill your feet to the bone before you even realized it. I laid back and pulled the covers up, reaching for the chain on the bedside lamp at the same time. The room was cast into darkness as the covers reached my chin.

As I began to settle into the comfort of my bed, the blue glow and faint buzz of my phone startled me. Frowning at the thought of the late hour, I groped blindly in the near darkness and grabbed my phone. With it still attached to the charging cable, I opened the message banner on the lock screen.

Hey, Si! Hope it's not too late. Any interest in this? It matches the paint in your house. Let me know when you see this!

The text from Max Nguyen was followed quickly by a photo of a green cupboard in his store. Before I could answer, another message slipped onto the screen.

It's free. Just gas money for delivery. Someone left it out front and I don't have the room for it right now. Business…is slow.

I couldn't help but half smile, half grimace, at the message. Business was *slow* everywhere in town. Tapping out a response quickly, I began imagining where the cupboard would look best in my house.

Fifty bucks sound good?

The response was nearly immediate.

Deal! Bring it by around eight tomorrow evening?

Deal.

Max responded to my text by giving it a thumbs up reaction emoji, but no more messages came through. Obviously, he knew he had been bothering me late in the evening, so he wasn't going to bother me further. I gave the cupboard picture a few more moments of inspection, then locked my phone and laid it back on the bedside table.

My eyes immediately felt heavy as I shifted happily against the mattress, finding the perfect position. Though my evening snack had left me groggy, and my body was prepared for sleep, my mind had other ideas. As I did my best to drift off, Chester's question was playing on repeat in my head.

What will you do now?

Working harder was always the answer. It was going to catch up to me eventually. With a sigh and the resolve to make things work, I was finally able to push the thought away, and I fell into a restful slumber.

CHAPTER 2

"So," Ginny was saying as I quartered tomatoes, "she said that I could write my paper about the *debated* existence of ghosts, but I'd likely get a bad grade."

I chuckled, glancing at the window out of the corner of my eye.

"But I told her that I actually *know* a medium," Ginny continued. "A famous one! I told her who you were, and that I volunteered here with you, and she knew who you were, but she said the same thing again!"

"Well—"

"And it's just ignorance, Si!" Ginny proclaimed as she started gathering up the tomatoes I'd chopped and began laying them on a baking sheet. "People are willfully and happily ignorant and won't open their minds to other thoughts and ideas. They can't even admit that *maybe* they aren't right about everything and that just because you can't see it doesn't make it not true."

"I—"

"A college professor of all people, too!" She howled as she began drizzling olive oil over the full sheet of tomatoes. "They should be the most open-minded people!"

When Ginny grabbed the salt and pepper to season the tomatoes, I stopped her.

"Well," I said quickly, reaching for a few jars of other spices, "I've told you a million times that most people think I'm a charlatan. And there's nothing you can do about that. Do yourself a favor and write your paper about one of the approved spiritual topics on the syllabus."

"Si, how can you say that? You're not a charlatan!"

I shrugged as she sprinkled salt and pepper on the tomatoes and I got festive with the paprika, garlic powder, onion powder, and a touch of cayenne. Four large sheet pans full of tomatoes were oiled, seasoned, and ready to roast. Glancing behind us at the two ovens, I saw that the preheat lights were still on. I turned my attention back to Ginny.

"I know I'm not a charlatan," I said, glancing at the front window of The Lunch Counter again. "But I can't make everyone believe it. I don't have the time—*or desire*—to deliver messages from dead relatives to everyone on Earth to prove anything. And even if I did, some people still wouldn't believe me. Too many charlatans ruined it for the rest of us. So…who cares?"

I shrugged again and turned to lean on the serving counter. My eyes darted to the front window once more. I couldn't help myself. The ghost that had followed me to work for the umpteenth day in a row was standing outside, staring at me. The name of The Lunch Counter is emblazoned in big, blue, block letters on the front window. In the center of the "o" in the painted name was the ghost's eyes, watching me. If I thought he'd done it intentionally, I would have been amused. Instead, I was unnerved.

The thing is, when you're a medium, and you see a ghost—meaning that you're also some level of clairvoyant—several things are happening at once. One, you can't really acknowledge the ghost, because then normies will think you're schizophrenic and call the police. Even if you explain you're a medium. Or maybe because you explain you're a medium.

Two, it makes it hard to focus on other, more important activities, because ghosts, for obvious reasons, pull focus. Three, whether you like it or not, being in the presence of a ghost when you're a medium, changes the vibe. And people notice. It's hard to act normal when things are not…normal.

Most importantly, and something a lot of people aren't aware of—*since most people are not mediums*—is that you don't often want to let ghosts know you see them. Once a ghost knows you are aware of their presence, they will follow you. Some try to tell you to find an alive person and deliver a message. Or complete some unfinished business for them. Some ghosts simply want someone to talk to because they're lonely. Some aren't verbal and stare like creeps, giving you an "ookie" feeling. Others simply wail and make noise.

The ghost at the window was already too aware of my abilities and was far too attached. I didn't need to make things worse.

If you've never tried to act normal while a ghost screams bloody murder next to your ear so that neither the ghost nor other people know you know there's a ghost nearby, you're lucky. Pretending to be normal when you're a medium is exhausting. When you're a clairvoyant medium, it's worse.

Even if you're a regionally semi-famous medium, such as myself, putting your best foot forward with others means the whole "medium thing" isn't your conversation opener. It's difficult to not acknowledge something that I was born with, like my race, ethnicity, sexuality, and hair and eye color. I'm a medium. I can't turn it off. Sometimes I find ghosts because my clients want me to call them forth. I get paid for that. Some ghosts figure out that I can see them and won't leave me alone until I help them. With that, comes a lot of problems.

Knockknockknock.

Hi. I'm Silas Erie. I came to see you because I can see ghosts and your great grandma Myrtle said she's disappointed you're still with your bum husband, Steven, and she wishes she had written you out of the will. Would you like to say something to her so that she can move on and stop following me around the store while I'm grocery shopping? That'd be great, thanks.

You can see how this would be a problem. Believer or not, many people don't take kindly to being approached in such a way. I find that most people who believe that I truly am capable of seeing ghosts would rather approach me. They don't want me to go all cuckoo and approach them while they're at the deli counter.

Excuse me. Do you know an older gentleman who died of a heart attack? Fella with a questionable haircut that's possibly a toupee and died with a blue cardigan on?

First of all, I wouldn't open with a leading question. I wouldn't approach someone like that, but I certainly wouldn't approach them if I wasn't certain the ghost I was dealing with belonged to them. That's simply rude. Why get someone worked up that you might have a message from the afterlife for them, but be wrong? No one wants grandpa's message from the beyond given to them while strangers eavesdrop, anyway. Especially since not all messages from beyond the grave are family friendly. Ghosts can be ratchet. Trust me. In death, decorum can completely go out the window, especially if the dead person wasn't exactly well-mannered in life.

Thinking about the struggles of being a medium, I nearly marched over to the front door to begin checking the corners for the silver pieces. I had to stop myself. All of the doors and windows in The Lunch Counter had silver in their corners to keep the ghosts from being able to enter. Like every door and window at my house. The paint on the walls and ceiling had been mixed with sage ash. Like every wall and ceiling at my house. My peace wasn't protected out in the real world, but at The Lunch Counter and at home, I was good.

"Where is it?" Ginny asked as the ovens behind us clicked.

I didn't have to look to know the preheat lights were off.

"Front window," I said. "He's a Traveler but not too much of a talker. He's been following me for a while. Just glad he's not a Screamer."

Ginny frowned and stared at the front window. I couldn't imagine how frustrating it had to be to have someone tell you they can see ghosts but you have nothing but your faith in them to make you believe it.

"Well," Ginny said, "if he gets feisty, you let me know. I'll go out there and start slinging holy water."

I couldn't help but laugh. Ginny gave me a sly wink when I pushed away from the counter, and together, we got the four trays put into the ovens. In thirty-five to forty minutes, we'd have perfectly roasted tomatoes to make the soup. Paired with made-on-the-fly grilled cheeses it would be the perfect lunch for our patrons.

"Good luck finding holy water," I said. "Nearest church is twenty miles away. And it doesn't work on ghosts, anyway. That's just a myth."

"You keep saying that, but I'm not sure I believe it."

"You believe I can see ghosts and talk to them, but you think I'm wrong about the holy water?" I asked, one eyebrow rising. "That's deranged."

Ginny chuckled as she set the timer for the ovens.

"Why wouldn't it work?" she asked. "It's *holy* water. If it can affect vampires—"

"Really?"

She shrugged. "—then why can't it hurt ghosts?"

"Because holy water is a religious thing. Being a ghost has nothing to do with religion. You're just…a ghost."

"That doesn't explain anything!" Ginny laughed.

"Ghosts have been around since man existed," I said with a laugh. "Religion came long after man started walking upright. Holy water is a religious thing. Ghosts are not."

"God existed before man, even if there wasn't religion."

"Debatable," I replied.

"Who says?"

"Everyone."

"Heretics!"

"Atheists, actually," I said. "Regardless, holy water is a human invention that came after the first existence of ghosts. They could care less about it."

"Then why does silver and sage keep them out of buildings, huh?" Ginny smiled proudly.

"Are you trying to insinuate that silver and sage are also human inventions that came after ghosts?" I laughed.

She rolled her eyes but dropped the topic. Ginny walked around the service counter and plopped down on one of the diner-style stools bolted to the floor in front of it. I stared at her from across the counter, amused.

The Lunch Counter was once the thriving 'Sage Grove Diner', serving hundreds of meals a day. Back when our little river-front town was a big shipping port on the Mississippi. Times change. As the shipping business tapered off and disappeared, the ports closed and the piers and docks were abandoned, then rotted and fell into the river, a similar fate fell upon our town. Sage Grove had seen better days, and a small stroll down the main thoroughfare proved it.

Except for the Wash-A-Teria, Shop-A-Teria, the Gas & Go, the post office, and The Lunch Counter, almost every business was shuttered. More than a third of the homes in the town of nine hundred and thirty-two people was abandoned. Many were at the point of needing to be condemned, but no officials were around to make those decisions. Our honorary mayor, David Honeycutt, had the authority to label any houses as condemned, but why would it matter? Who was he going to send to tear them down and clear out the debris? Sage Grove barely had a budget to keep the one street light working and the mail delivered, the water running, and the roads in decent condition.

When I'd bought and opened The Lunch Counter, I was fortunate enough to find that it was one of the buildings in town that had not completely fallen into disrepair. The plumbing and electrical were good and most of the repairs that needed to be done were minor or aesthetic. It took a little money and some work, but my profits from my medium business, and a bit of know-how and elbow grease, took care of those problems. Within six weeks of purchasing the place, I had it open and ready for business.

Now, you may be asking yourself why someone who makes a decent living as a medium would open a diner. Additionally, you may be asking why *anyone* would open a diner on a rundown street in a rundown town with a population of less than a thousand people. It's the same reason I'd been applying for the Waterson Altruism Grant for three consecutive years. Someone had to help feed the unhoused and poverty-stricken residents of Sage Grove. The town couldn't afford to do it. The local and state governments weren't interested in helping, either, preferring to ignore and wait the problem out.

With the money I put into The Lunch Counter from my medium business, everyone in town who needs it gets at least one decent meal a day. Obviously, we never have the money to serve anything elaborate, but a hot sandwich and a bowl of soup go a long way when you're talking about people with daily food insecurity. Without the Waterson Altruism Grant, that was the best I could do while still taking care of my own needs. However, it was my goal to one day have enough donations and grants coming in so that everyone in town who needed it was guaranteed three meals a day.

The bell jangling over the door brought me out of my thoughts once again. Ginny spun on the stool slowly to see who had entered as I looked up from my spot behind the counter. I didn't even have a chance to say a word before Ginny was standing up and putting her hands on her hips.

"It's four dollars or whatever you can afford—*including free.* Now get out of here, Gary!"

I shook my head at the sight of the man ducking out of the front entrance, the door gliding shut behind him. Following him with my eyes, he dashed right past the front window, passing through the ghost who was still staring at me through the "O" on the glass. Gary shivered when he passed through the ghost, but gave no other indication that he noticed it. I tore my eyes away before they connected with the ghost's. I didn't want to encourage him.

"Every single day, Si." Ginny sighed, shaking her head. "Gary has been coming in here every day, saying nothing, just staring like a lunatic. Does he think anything is going to change? And he knows Sal is going to pick up enough for everyone at the camp anyway."

"You're too mean to him," I said, admonishing her as I slid my phone from my hip pocket. "Other than everyone at the camp, he doesn't have anyone. He misses being a part of society."

"Then come in and start a real conversation!" Ginny exclaimed.

I glanced at my phone screen.

"I gotta skedaddle," I said. "It's almost time for Rhonda."

Ginny shook her head with a smile.

"She hasn't given up?" she asked. "After all this time?"

"I don't think she ever will," I replied, rounding the counter. "Not until she's dead, anyway. Then she won't need me. It's only been a couple months, anyhow. That's not too long to grieve."

"She doesn't need you now. You haven't been able to summon her husband, and it's been forever!"

"Hey," I said, passing by Ginny on the stool, "she pays me fifty bucks every day to come try to contact the guy. That's a lot of tomato soup and grilled cheese sandwiches for everyone. I'll keep trying as long as she keeps paying."

Ginny eyed me for a moment when I turned at the front door to grin at her.

"Maybe you are a charlatan, Si," she said. "Because any respectable medium would have told her to give up the ghost by now. *Ha! Give up the ghost!*"

I rolled my eyes.

"Very clever," I groaned. "I'll be back in time to help serve. You good on blending up soup ingredients and getting everything ready?"

"Aren't I always?"

"Victor Grimm wouldn't have told her to give up," I murmured.

"I said *respectable medium*," Ginny said.

I winked at my helper and dashed out the front door. Fortunately, with it being late morning in early fall, it hadn't been necessary to grab my coat or a hat before ducking out of work. A cool autumnal breeze was whistling down the street, ruffling my hair, but it wasn't anything I couldn't handle. As I walked past the ghost at the window, he turned, wordlessly, and fell in behind me. Floating along behind me, he said nothing, and I pretended to not notice.

We'd already spoken once, and that was enough. I wasn't able to help him. He needed to move along. Until he chose to do so, I was going to ignore him—and I didn't care how long I had to ignore him to prove I was a man of my word.

Gary was in the little alcove between the side of The Lunch Counter and the Wash-A-Teria. He was turned so that I could only see his profile, and he had his arms wrapped around himself—a self-soothing gesture. When I came up alongside him, I stopped and turned to face him, but kept my distance. Gary didn't like being touched or to have his personal bubble invaded.

For as long as The Lunch Counter had been open, Gary had been one of the daily faces. He'd sneak in the front door, quiet as a church mouse, wearing his brown trousers and black sneakers that had seen better days, along with a ratty t-shirt and a cardigan that was two sizes too big. He'd asked one question, as quietly as he could while still being heard. *How much for a meal?*

It didn't matter that our prices had not changed over the three years The Lunch Counter had been open. It didn't matter that the leader of the homeless camp, Sal, would always be the one to come pick up meals for the folks at the camp. It didn't matter that the cost didn't actually matter—if a person needed a meal, *they got a meal.* Gary came in every day and asked the cost every day. And every day I gave him the same answer. However, sometimes Ginny would snap at him, annoyed with answering the same question every day.

But he hadn't actually spoke in quite a while. He had turned into more of a silent creeper lately.

Gary was on the taller side, and obviously in need of the meal he got each day from us. A "bean pole," most people would call him. Hunched in the shadow of the space between the two buildings, the hem of his cardigan flapping in the breeze, he looked small. Like a wounded bird.

"You didn't do anything wrong, Gary," I said. "Don't beat yourself up too much about it."

He nodded nervously, avoiding eye contact. His hands flexed, gripping his flesh tightly as he hugged himself. I looked in the direction I'd been going, not wanting to be late, but not wanting to ignore someone in obvious crisis.

"Are you going to be okay?" I asked.

He nodded furiously again.

"Do you need me to walk with you back to the camp?" I asked.

Gary shook his head, though a little more calmly.

"Okay," I said. "Head back when you feel like it. Sal will come get food for everyone. I'll make sure she gets a sandwich and soup for you. I promise. All right?"

Gary made eye contact then, but only briefly. Then he looked down and nodded. He seemed as if he wanted to say something, but was holding back. Since I couldn't force the man to speak to me, I let it go. A smile played at the corner of his mouth briefly. I smiled back.

"Good," I said. "See you tomorrow, Gary."

He nodded.

I said nothing else as I turned away from Gary, leaving him in the shadowy cocoon between the two buildings, and carried on my way. Making sure Gary was okay had been my goal, and I had achieved it. Even though I desperately wanted to talk to

Gary more, possibly delving into the reasons behind his situation and behaviors, I knew it was pointless. Gary didn't tolerate intrusions from others well—physical or otherwise. Leaving him to collect himself before he headed back to camp was all I could do.

Rhonda Milner's house wasn't far from The Lunch Counter, so I never saw a reason to drive from one to the other. The short physical space between the two structures paled in comparison to the economic distance. The Lunch Counter, though in much better shape than the other dilapidated businesses in Sage Grove, looked like a shack compared to the Milner abode.

Within a minute of leaving Gary at the side of The Lunch Counter, I was trudging down the sidewalk to the front gate of the house. Whether iron works on ghosts like the legends say it works on the fae, I'm not sure. However, when I grabbed the iron gate and swung it open enough to slip into the front courtyard, the ghost following me fell back. Once the gate clanged shut, the ghost moved up, keeping a yard of space between himself and the gate, and watched me as I continued up the stone walkway to the front porch. It was the same thing he'd done every day I'd walked over to give Rhonda Milner her daily reading.

Keeping my eyes ahead and not glancing over my shoulder at the ghost was difficult, but I managed. I stared at the house as I walked the path and took the steps up to the huge wrap-around porch. At the door, I made sure to use the doormat for its intended purpose, stomping my feet when I was done to make sure my shoes were thoroughly clean. Then I took a deep breath, sighed, mentally preparing myself for the reading ahead of me, and pushed the doorbell.

Muffled chimes sounded in the home beyond, and I kept my eyes on the imposing, polished oak door as I waited. After what seemed like an eternity, I heard movement in the house, the sound of high heels on wood. Hours seemed to pass by as the person made their way through the gargantuan house, and then I heard the clicking of locks. Finally, the door swung wide.

And the screams began.

CHAPTER 3

"*Oh-my-goodness-Silas-I'm-so-glad-to-see-you!*"

Rhonda Milner's arms shot out to pull me into a—not necessarily desired—hug as we stood in the doorway of her mansion. As a kind person, a professional—*and mostly as a guy with bills to pay*—I accepted the hug, reaching up to rest my hands lightly against her back. Briefly. When Rhonda pulled away, her unnaturally white veneers on high beam, I returned her smile. She grabbed my hands in hers and pulled me into her home.

Closing the door with the swivel of an elegant hip, swathed in a pencil skirt comprised of a material I probably couldn't afford, Rhonda dragged me towards The Parlor. Her silk blouse was cool against my arm as she laced hers through mine. The Parlor was the room at the front of her house that most normal people would call the living room, but was actually that what rich people called…The Parlor. Basically, a rich person's front room where they entertain those guests that they feel are not worthy of being invited into the innermost parts of their house.

"Oh, Silas!" Rhonda cooed as she pulled me into the room. "I had a dream last night! A *prophetic* dream!"

"Oh?"

She pulled me over to the sofas that faced each other.

"Yes!" She practically shoved me onto one sofa and lowered herself onto the one across from me. "Last night, I went to sleep—and slept like a baby for the first time in months! My dream told me that today is the day that Harlan will finally speak to us!"

Forcing myself to not grumble uncomfortably, I repositioned myself on the sofa and laid my hands on my knees. Rhonda was smoothing out the nonexistent wrinkles in her skirt as she settled into the couch, her eyes focused elsewhere. I took a moment to assess The Parlor. She'd added more candles. The temperature in the room, compared to the grand foyer, was noticeably higher. A cough nearly escaped my throat as I did my best not to pull at the collar of my shirt. Rhonda seemed unbothered by the oppressive warmth put off by the candles in the space.

Cozy spaces during autumn are one of my favorite things, but Rhonda's front room was pushing the limit. Warm, fuzzy blankets in front of a fire was a vibe I could enjoy. Roasting in the pits of Hell for all of my sins was not. Of course, I wasn't actually certain Hell even existed. If there are so many spirits hanging around, I was beginning to believe they had nowhere to go until their business was finished. After that, well, I had no idea what happened to ghosts I stopped seeing after a time.

"Well," I said slowly, "that's definitely something, right?"

Rhonda was bobbing her head like she was glued to a car's dashboard. Certainty that a loved one who has passed is trying to reach us from beyond the grave is not a unique experience. Everyone I've ever known—including myself—has done their best to find signs in everything from dust patterns on their credenzas to dreams to scorch marks on their toast.

As an authentic and professional medium and clairvoyant, I do my best to comfort the grieving and help them the best I can. Ease them into acceptance that their loved one is never going to return, even if they are still possibly lingering around in a plane of existence most can't see or fathom. It's much better than telling them they're batshit crazy, after all.

First things first, most ghosts are not powerful enough to physically manifest some evidence of their existence. Secondly, the greater majority of the human population will go their entire life without ever realizing they've had a ghostly experience. Around ninety-five percent of the people who have actually had an experience with the deceased chalked it up to drowsiness, inebriation, hallucination, or some natural phenomenon they can't quite explain.

Because of these first two points, most people don't believe that I, an actual medium who can see ghosts, is actually seeing ghosts. They certainly don't believe I can commune with them. So, getting someone to believe I have a message, then convincing them to receive the message so the ghost can drop their mission, is an uphill battle. Worst of all, if the person finally comes around and accepts the message, and that it's genuine, they tend to begin to believe that they can then commune with their ghostly loved one as much as they want moving forward. When I try to explain it doesn't work like that—though I have no idea why ghosts lose interest or disappear after delivering certain messages—they once again accuse me of being a charlatan. It's a no-win situation sometimes, being a medium.

Thirdly, and possibly worst of all, is finding a true believer like Rhonda Milner and having to tell her that her loved one simply isn't showing up when called. Sometimes, though it's rare, certain ghosts have no interest in being summoned to deliver a message to a loved one. Maybe they're not around any longer and have *moved on*. It's possible they have no interest in the person for whom you are summoning them. A lack of message to give to the person in question might be another reason a ghost fails to show up. Or the ghost might simply not want to talk to the person for personal reasons.

Ghosts can hold grudges. Once you slip away from your humanly form to your spiritual existence, your personality doesn't simply disappear. If cousin Ricky stole your BMX when you were twelve and never apologized, you may carry that grudge to the afterlife. To hell with cousin Ricky. Y'all can settle up once he joins you in the spirit dimension, I suppose?

When it came to Rhonda Milner, it was clear that her deceased husband was never going to show up when I came to her house to summon him. That wasn't simply negativity or professional experience talking—we'd been trying for months. Harlan Milner had decided, for his own reasons, that he did not want to talk to his wife once he'd died. I could call him all day and night, but I couldn't force him to deliver a message to someone if he didn't want to do it.

The money kept flowing from Rhonda's pocketbook to my wallet to the coffers of The Lunch Counter, so I had no plans to give up. As long as Rhonda wanted to keep trying, I'd keep coming to her house as many times a week as she wanted to call for Harlan Milner to come talk to his wife. As frustrating as it was to put on a show so often for Rhonda, it helped fund an important cause. Continuing to show up and do my best was my plan for the foreseeable future, even if I knew there was no point in any of it.

"Maybe we try a different relative today?" I cleared my throat and sat forward on the sofa. "A grandparent? Cousin? A parent? Maybe a friend?"

Rhonda was shaking her head before I could finish my questions.

"I want to talk to Harlan," Rhonda stated firmly. "My dream told me that today is the day. Now, if anyone else shows up, that's fine. But I want to keep trying."

"Okay," I said evenly. "I'll do my best, but—"

"I know you're trying, Silas," Rhonda said, reaching across to take my hand and give it a brief, reassuring squeeze. "He'll show up when he feels the time is right."

I gave a one shoulder shrug and produced my most boyish grin for Rhonda.

"It's your time and money," I said. "I certainly won't tell you how to spend either."

Her smile lit up the room once more.

"Excellent!"

After meeting Rhonda's eyes and giving her another smile, I eased back into the sofa and took a deep breath. Rhonda perched on the edge of her sofa and watched me with an intensity I'd become familiar with over the months. Taking a deep breath and shaking my head as if to clear my thoughts— mostly for show—I finally spoke.

"I'm here to commune with the spirit realm," I said, trying not to laugh at myself. "I call on Harlan Milner, if he is here, to step through the veil and speak with me on behalf of his beloved wife, Rhonda Milner."

Harlan wasn't going to show up, I already knew that. However, I closed my eyes and pretended to concentrate on summoning him. For Rhonda's sake. After several tense moments, I opened my eyes and looked around.

No Harlan. Again.

However, it hadn't been a total waste. There was one ghost in the corner of The Parlor, tapping her foot, her arms crossed over her chest. The thin, elderly woman with a chignon of white hair, wearing what looked like a Chanel suit, looked ready to clutch her pearls. She was staring directly at me, probably appalled that I was sitting on such a nice sofa in jeans and a t-shirt and a secondhand jacket.

"No Harlan," I said with an exhale as I looked over at Rhonda.

She slumped slightly, her shoulders collapsing as her eyes went to her lap.

"Your mother is here again," I said.

Rhonda's demeanor changed immediately. She gripped her knees and her head lifted, a glower on her face. Through gritted teeth, she muttered a reply.

"*I will not speak to that woman. Even in death.*"

I shrugged. "Your dime."

Looking over Rhonda's shoulder, I made eye contact with the apparition of her mother.

"She still doesn't to talk to you," I said.

'*I CAN HEAR HER!*' Her mother's ghost wailed.

Shrugging, I said, "Okay. Well, she doesn't want to hear anything you have to say. Sorry."

Rhonda, watching me closely, fascinated by my one-sided conversation, was sitting on the edge of the sofa.

"Maybe some other time we can—" I began.

"*I will never speak to her,*" Rhonda insisted from the other sofa.

The ghost in the corner looked at the back of Rhonda's head and flipped her the bird. Then she gave me one for good measure. And she was gone. My eyes went back to Rhonda.

"She's nice," I said simply.

Rhonda chuckled. "I don't want to know."

"You know," I said slowly, "it's possible she'll never, um, *move on*, if you don't hear what she has to say. She might keep lingering around here until—"

"Let her suffer." Rhonda sniffed, going rigid. "She would have done the same to me."

I examined my client for a moment. It had to be a difficult life, being unable to let go of the past and hurt caused by others. But I was a medium, not a therapist.

"Totally up to you," I said.

"Can we try again?" Rhonda asked. "Just once more?"

"You have me for an hour," I said. "I can keep calling to Harlan as long as I'm on the clock."

Rhonda smiled. "Good!"

Regardless of Rhonda's optimistic outlook on all things related to her husband's spirit, the rest of the hour proved to be fruitless. Once her allotted time was up, I was once again faced with giving Rhonda the bad news. Harlan Milner, her husband who had passed away four months prior, was still a no show. His interest in speaking directly with his widow was nonexistent. Fortunately, Rhonda took the news as well as she did in every other session, and thanked me profusely for my time. Furthermore, she had allowed me to pass along a message from a long-lost cousin who decided to show up during the session, so it wasn't a complete waste of time.

As Rhonda was showing me out the front door moments after the session had ended—*no point in letting The Help linger*— all evidence of spirit was gone from her house. One thing to know about spirits—they're almost everywhere at all times. As a medium, I find that discovering a space where a spirit doesn't wander through from time to time is unusual. Rhonda Milner's house was one such space. Unless I was present, calling out to spirits, her house seemed to be a crypt. I shivered as I stepped out of the house, thinking about how quiet the place must be for a widow.

"Now," Rhonda said, filling the doorway to speak to me as I turned to her, "I'll see you again tomorrow?"

Seeing her small frame take up the entire entryway was an obvious message. Unless I was there on business, I wasn't welcome. Rhonda Milner was actually, regardless of all her niceties and pleasantries, an elitist. I was a poor young man who spoke to spirits and ran a charity for the hungry.

You do not belong here unless you are being paid, Rhonda's position in her doorway announced.

"It's Friday," I said. "See you Monday?"

Rhonda reached up and laid a delicate hand against the side of her head and grinned, her eyes sliding shut dramatically.

"Of course, of course!" She chuckled.

"But I will see you on Monday," I replied.

Rhonda opened her eyes, her mouth sliding open to respond, but the sound of a truck engine and tires on pavement stopped her short. Her gaze shifted to the gate that led into the driveway that ran alongside the house. Turning on my heels to check things out for myself, I immediately recognized the dual-cab pickup that was waiting for the tall wrought-iron gate to slide out of the way and admit entrance.

Before anything could be said, I turned back to Rhonda and gave her a nod of my head.

"Well," I said, "since you have company, I'll be on my way. Crossed fingers for next time!"

Rhonda glanced back at me, smiled, and held up a pair of crossed fingers, her attention not really on me. I turned away once again and dashed across the porch at a pace that, I hoped, didn't read as panic. I skipped down the steps, doing my best to keep my eyes forward, on the path towards the gate, as I made my way from the house.

Never one to leave well enough alone, once the driveway gate was fully open, and the truck was pulling up the drive, I couldn't help but glance over. Without even trying, my eyes connected with the truck driver's and I quickly whipped my head back around. A second later, I was at the gate, and I pushed it open and dashed through, making my escape.

I made sure the gate closed behind me, but I kept my eyes on anything but Rhonda's house, the driveway, the truck, and its driver. Once I was certain that it was shut securely behind me, I dashed down the sidewalk and away from my client's house. The money that Rhonda Milner tossed at me five days a week to try and summon her dead husband was a boon for The Lunch Counter. However, it wasn't enough to deal with some things that came with being her client.

So, like an adult, I avoided those things.

CHAPTER 4

"Hey!"

Ignoring the man hollering from behind me, I powerwalked away from the Milner abode, feigning sudden deafness. The fact that the ghost that had followed me to Rhonda's was pacing me, wailing at the side of my head, helped the illusion. When a ghost is screaming in your ear, it's easier to pretend that one is distracted—because one is actually distracted. Of course, no one except another medium could have been sure of that fact. Regardless, I used it to my advantage.

"Silas!"

I continued along the sidewalk through town, away from the mansion, though I knew it was all in vain. Eventually, the man behind me was going to catch up. If not, he'd follow me all the way back to The Lunch Counter if necessary. Between the sounds of the wailing ghost and the man's screams behind me, it quickly became apparent that I was fighting a losing battle. Once I'd reached the corner of Main Street, I quickly turned, then picked up my pace once I was certain I was out of view of Rhonda's home.

Getting out of sight didn't stop the man's hollers of protestation behind me. But with the help of the ghost's wails as it raced along beside me, I was able to filter out the screams that rapidly faded away behind me. By the time I ducked through the front door of The Lunch Counter a minute later, and blocking the ghost from further access to me, I'd nearly forgotten the entire encounter.

Ginny was standing at the stove, two giant soup pots on the burners before her. She was moving an immersion blender around in one of the pots, whirring noises filling the space, as she prepared the tomato soup. As I expected, I'd been gone long enough for the sheets of tomatoes to fully roast. Ginny had already transferred them, the onions, and the garlic into the pots and was blending them up into soup.

Having been to the rodeo a time or two before, I went to the pantry and grabbed a couple quarts of chicken stock. Another stop at the fridge to grab the quart of cream, and I joined Ginny at the stove. As she blended the simmering concoction, I added chicken stock to thin it to an appropriate consistency. Then I added cream to, well, make it creamy.

Working in tandem for a few minutes, we soon had two huge pots of steamy, creamy tomato soup, ready to serve. Ginny set the lids to the pots, leaving them slightly ajar as I put away supplies and cleaned the immersion blender. As I returned to the prep counter next to the stove, Ginny was laying slices of bread on the freshly cleaned surface. I grabbed the margarine tub and pre-sliced cheese from the fridge and jumped in to help.

"So," Jenny began as she laid out bread in rows, "did Mr. Milner decide to make an appearance, or are we getting more grocery money from Rhonda for another week?"

"We'll be able to make more tomato soup and grilled cheese sandwiches for a bit longer," I said.

Ginny cackled, then grew pensive.

"I mean, I'm glad we are still going to have her as a *donor* and all, but this is so odd for you, Si," she said. "You hardly ever fail."

I shrugged and retrieved a knife to spread the butter-like substance on the bread slices.

"Be honest with me," Ginny murmured, "are you playing the long game with ole girl or what? You've been at this with her for months."

I couldn't help but laugh at the notion, though Ginny's question made me nervous.

"I'm not swindling my best client," I replied as I slathered bread with margarine. "Mr. Milner never shows up when I'm trying to summon him at the house."

"That's so odd. Right? I mean, you get clients contacting you from all over the world and you're almost always able to give them...*something*."

My shoulders rose and fell again of their own volition.

There's one difficult aspect to being a medium that no one ever discusses—probably because there aren't many people to talk to about it. If you fail to produce results for someone wanting you to contact a deceased loved one, your entire career—*all of your abilities*—are suddenly placed under a microscope. If a single ghost decides it doesn't want to play your game, you suddenly suck at your job. Even if there were tons of people to talk to about this aspect of the profession, I'm not certain that I would. Giving other mediums a reason to doubt your abilities is how rumors about you being a grifter begin.

"I can't control the ghosts," I said. "I can only call 'em."

Ginny frowned, the middle of her forehead becoming a canyon of a crease.

"I know it's not your fault, Si, it's just that—"

The front door of The Lunch Counter whipped open and a whirling dervish breezed through the front door. My coworker grinned broadly at the sight of Sal's taupe-colored flowing skirt twirling around her like a tornado. A royal blue broad brimmed summer hat—of all things—perched atop her flaming locks, refusing to move. Her royal blue jersey-knit shirt and taupe blazer tied the look together and the dangly stone earrings hanging from her ears topped it off. No one would have pegged her as the unofficial leader of the homeless camp, unless they knew her.

Seemingly put together, it was the minor details one had to inspect to tell Sal wasn't a woman of means. The clumpy lipstick and mascara, the ripped seam here and there, the fact that the earrings didn't quite match, and shoes that needed replacing were the biggest clues. Of course, I had known Sal for years, so no one had to clue me in to the fact that she was unhoused.

"I'd like to say that it's a beautiful day, but it's colder than ice water poured down Frosty's buttcrack into an aluminum tumbler out there!" Sal proclaimed with a flourish of her head.

Ginny cackled and I chuckled at her display as we continued to work on the grilled cheeses. My first instinct was to tell Sal it wasn't all that cold. I'd been out in it on my walk to Rhonda's house, after all. However, Sal lived in a ramshackle shed down at the homeless encampment with no central heat that barely kept the elements outside. Telling her it wasn't that cold outside would have been like telling any Midwesterner that Jello doesn't belong in a salad.

"How ya' doin', Sal?" I asked.

I indicated to Ginny to start grilling the cheeses as I grabbed a towel to wipe my hands. My partner got the griddle heating and began assembling sandwiches to grill up for Sal and her folks down at the camp.

"How many sandwiches today?"

"I'm good as can be expected," Sal said, digging in the tiny purse slung messenger style over her neck. "Didn't wake up dead again, so thank God for small miracles."

"For sure," I replied.

Her hand came out of her purse with a collection of crumpled bills and a bit of change, which she held out to me. Seeing the sad collection of money, I desperately wanted to refuse it. However, Sal was still a human being with dignity and pride, so I politely held my cupped hands out to her, and she deposited the wad of money in them. Without bothering to sort or count it, I slid it under the counter for later attention.

"How many can you spare?" Sal asked.

I washed my hands in the sink since handling money and then food isn't the wisest choice.

"I asked how many you needed," I said, turning to her as I dried my hands on a towel.

Sal eyed me for a moment, but knew she'd be fighting a losing battle.

"Well," she said finally, "we got a full house lately. People aren't doing good. Not lately. You know how things are."

I nodded. "How many?"

"We got me, Susie-Q, Ronnie Boy, Gary—"

"Sal," I stopped her, "you don't have to justify the need. I just need a number."

She chewed at the corner of her lip for a moment, transferring some of the lipstick to her canine. After a long moment, she finally came up with a number.

"Sixteen," she said. "If the money will cover it."

"Your money is always good here, Sal," I said. "You want a few extras in case?"

Sal eyed me once again, then, with rosy cheeks, looked down at the floor and nodded.

"I don't expect we'll have many today," I said, ignoring her embarrassment. "The customers get fewer and fewer as more people move out of town."

"Not much keeping them here," Sal said, glad to have something to talk about besides the needs of the camp. "Every building in town will be abandoned before you know it. Sage Grove really will be a ghost town one day."

We exchanged a knowing grin, and I turned to help Ginny with the order for the camp. Once I'd filled enough eight-ounce deli containers of soup and slapped lids tightly on them, I stacked them on the counter next to the stove and turned back to Sal. Propping my elbows on the counter, I leaned in to talk to Sal. Taking my cue, she leaned in to hear me better.

"Caleb told me yesterday that Doc Stephens' old office building was checked by the county officers last night. They won't be by there again for at least a week. Probably a month, if we're honest."

Sal glanced over my shoulder at Ginny, then looked me in the eyes.

"I still don't trust Caleb. There's something about him…"

"I trust him. And you trust me. Dr. Stephens' office."

We locked eyes, staring at each other for several moments, before Sal gave an imperceptible nod of her head. I smiled and pushed back from the counter before Ginny could notice our exchange.

"Speaking of everyone out at the camp," Jenny began, giving me a start, "let me tell you about Gary, Sal."

A glance over my shoulder and I found she was removing sandwiches from the griddle. I dashed over to begin wrapping the hot sandwiches in parchment paper. Ginny finished stacking the sandwiches next to the griddle for me to wrap, then turned to waggle her spatula at Sal.

"If he doesn't stop coming in here every day to stare at Silas like a creep, I'm going to—"

"Oh, Ginny." Sal chuckled.

"I mean it," Ginny said, though without even looking at her, I could hear the amusement in her voice. "It's weird. He comes in here and says nothing. Just stares. He used to at least say…*something*…but now he doesn't. I ran him off before he could do it today."

"Ginny," Sal said, "you know he barely talked before. Since Marcella came up missing, he's been completely mute. You should be nice to him. God knows the man suffers."

"I don't care. He—"

"He's a homeless man with no friends, save us campers, and no family I know of." Sal stopped her. "He's doing the best he can."

Ginny sighed heavily. She turned back to put more sandwiches down on the griddle.

"Fine," she replied.

I wrapped the last sandwich and began putting the ready soup and the finished sandwiches in a large paper bag for Sal. Ginny had one more round to finish on the griddle before Sal would have her order. Within the next five minutes, Ginny and I had gotten Sal's order together and I was sliding the bag across the counter to her. She made a production of tightly wrapping her inadequate scarf around her neck before lifting the bag off the counter to cradle with one arm.

"Bring the deli containers back if you want to help us save money." I reminded her. "We can wash them up and reuse them for y'all."

Sal gave me a nod and stood up straight. With a puff of her chest, she said, "Back into the fray I go!"

With that, she left the shop, as much a tornado as she arrived.

"That woman," Ginny said, shaking her spatula at the door, "is something else."

I went back to work to help her get more sandwiches ready to fire as needed. Over the next few hours, Ginny and I grilled sandwiches and ladled soup into to-go containers for the residents of Sage Grove. Our clientele typically consisted of the unhoused, disabled, and elderly citizens who found cooking for themselves difficult. However, due to the blustery weather, we had several people come in to get a cheap, easy lunch that they ate at the counter as they visited with us and we cooked.

Though the flow of patrons was sporadic, and we never hit a chaotic moment, the time seemed to pass in the blink of an eye. Before I knew it, the soup pot was down to the dregs and we'd run out of bread. Fortunately, the sun was nearly set outside, a pinkish-purple sky aglow with the last rays of light. Everyone knew we only served lunch, so we'd have no more patrons for the rest of the day.

Being the types to clean as the day went by, there was little to take care of as we set about closing up The Lunch Counter for the day. With only a few dishes and utensils to wash, and counters and griddle to wipe down, the jobs would be complete before we knew it.

"I can finish the cleaning," Ginny announced as she wiped her hands on her apron with finality. "If you need to get out of here and get a headstart on the nightly dark workings."

I rolled my eyes.

"I mean, I could use extra time to work on internet requests," I said. "And Max is bringing a cupboard out tonight he thought I might like. So…yeah. I'll take you up on that."

I pulled the hand towel I had tucked into my waist of my pants out and tossed it at Ginny. She caught it in the air and growled playfully at me.

"Sorry," said. "I'm full of dark workings."

Seconds later, I was being chased out of my own diner by the whip cracks of a hand towel behind me. Ginny was glaring at me through the window of The Lunch Counter as I slid into my car and buckled myself in safely. I gave Ginny a wave, which she begrudgingly returned as I pulled away from the diner. The ghost that had been following me for months leapt into the car and took a seat next to me.

I'd become accustomed to this behavior and simply ignored him as I drove down to the gas station. Less than a minute later, I'd screeched to a stop outside the Gas & Go, and leapt from the car. Even slamming my door behind me, I knew I was doing nothing to dissuade, or stop, the ghost from following me. So, I continued to ignore him as I walked through the encroaching night to the store.

Caleb was at the checkout counter by the front door when I entered, yawning into a fist, but managed to give me a polite wave with his other hand as I breezed by. I gave him a polite nod and headed to the coolers, the ghost moaning and groaning as it floated behind me. Though we have a small grocery store in town, if I need something simple, I usually stop at the gas station if I'm on my way home. In and out in under two minutes is more my speed. Additionally, Caleb isn't too much of a talker, which makes picking up a carton of milk at the gas station much more pleasant.

After making my selection, I made my way back up to the front of the small store, milk in hand, ghost on my heels. Caleb gave me a curious look, but said nothing, as I set the carton on the counter before him. He glanced at the front window of the store and blinked at the last bit of light coming over the horizon, then turned his attention to my transaction.

"Not enough sleep for the night shift again?" I chuckled as Caleb rang me up.

"Never enough to deal with the harsh light of day," he said.

I laughed at his joke.

"Four-twenty-seven," Caleb said.

I grimaced as I reached for my wallet, which amused him.

"Grocery store is cheaper," he said as he took the five-dollar bill I passed him.

"But then I wouldn't get the ambience of the gas station," I replied.

Grinning, he made change, and held the coins out to me as I slid the quart of milk from counter. I shook my head and nodded at the jar on the counter labeled as donations for the local unhoused population. Caleb deposited the coins into the jar, the clinking sounds my soundtrack as I headed to the door.

"Thanks," I turned to say as I pushed the door open with my hip.

"See ya' next time," Caleb replied.

The ghost rode along with me all the way home, moaning from time to time, sometimes saying things that actually made sense. As always, I ignored it, though I knew it knew that I could see and hear it. It had been so long, being bothered by the ghost that I wasn't certain it'd ever give up. However, from past experience, I knew everyone—even ghosts—had their limit. Eventually, it would tire of its efforts with me and go out in a search of someone else who might help it.

Regardless, it'd find no help from me. No matter how long it could last, I could last longer.

By the time I was pulling down the road to my house, night had settled in Sage Grove, and the stars were beginning to twinkle in the velvety darkness above. Even from the end of the drive, as my headlights slashed across the start of the path, I could see the truck. I uttered something between a frustrated growl and resigned sigh as pulled down the drive towards the house.

When I pulled up to the front of the Craftsman-style home, I saw the shadow of a man sitting in one of the chairs on the front porch. I took my time parking the car next to the truck, shutting off the lights, grabbing the milk, and exiting the vehicle. The ghost fluttered from the car and went to float near the front door of the house. Like every other night, it was going to attempt entry when I opened the door, only to find its efforts fruitless.

Leaves and needles shed from the oaks and pines around the house crunched underfoot as I walked the path up to the porch. I had the sudden urge to ignore the man on the porch and head directly into the house, but I knew it wouldn't make him go away. He'd simply follow me. So, I shuffled up to the door, unlocked and popped it open, and reached around door jamb, feeling for the switch to the porchlight. The ghost did its best to jet through the open door, but bounced back several yards to float in the yard with an angry look on its face. I grinned to myself at its expression as my hand connected with the switch and flipped it up.

Yellow light flooded the front porch and I finally made direct eye contact with Danny Milner. One leg was laid over the over and his hands were clasped in his lap, as though he was trying to appear nonchalant. However, after I'd run from him earlier, I knew he was more…uh, *chalant?*…than he was letting on at the moment.

"I told you stay away from my mother," he said as he blinked rapidly in the sudden light.

"And I've told you to stay out of my business," I replied, holding the milk at my side. "I guess we both have cotton in our ears."

"I don't care if you want to swindle everyone else in the entire world, Si," Danny said calmly. "But leave my mother alone."

I sighed.

"Go home, Danny," I said. "We've had this discussion. Your mother is a grown woman, and—"

Danny was suddenly out of the chair and standing in front of me, his chest nearly touching mine. If he had wanted to startle or intimidate me, he'd have to try harder.

"A grown, *grieving* woman who would pay any amount of money to speak to her husband again," he grumbled.

"Almost anyone would pay any mount to speak to a dead loved one again," I said. "However, my rates are very reasonable."

"I'm telling you for the last time, Si—"

"Your mother could pay me to come and try to summon your father every day for the rest of her life and still be buried in a coffin made of bricks of hundreds." I stopped him. "And since most of that money goes into feeding the homeless around here, I think that's a fair trade. Anyway, your mother was hiring me from time to time to do silly little seances for her and her friends long before your father passed. If your mother wants me to stop coming around, she'll tell me herself. In fact, has she told you she wants me to stop coming? I know you've complained to her, too."

"She tells me to mind my business." Danny grumbled again, but made no move to give me space.

I gestured vaguely with my free hand.

"You are so annoying!" Danny growled.

"And you never know when to quit," I shrugged. "Now, can I help you with anything else, or—"

Before I could snip off another quip, Danny's hands were pulling me in and his mouth was covering mine. I wrapped my free arm around his back without hesitation and returned the deep, passionate kiss. Danny moaned as he pressed his body against mine and kissed me in a way that made it feel as if he was trying to soak up the essence of me. My eyes fluttered opened, and out in the yard, I could see the ghost staring at us.

"Inside," I managed to mumble around Danny's mouth.

He pushed me backwards into the house and kicked the door closed with the heel of his shoe. Doing my best to not stumble, I kept one arm around Danny as he pushed me from the door over to the sofa, his lips not leaving mine until he shoved me down onto the sofa. He was shucking off his jacket and climbing on top of me when I remembered something.

"The milk!" I exclaimed.

"Screw the milk," Danny muttered as he lowered himself towards me.

"I paid five bucks for it," I grinned goofily as I held it up to him.

Danny, growling with frustration, took the milk from my hand and disappeared into the kitchen. As the sound of the fridge opening and closing sounded, I stripped off my jacket and tossed it into my comfy chair. When Danny returned, he immediately leapt on top of me on the sofa and smothered my mouth with his again.

"I'm still not going to stop seeing your mom," I mumbled around Danny's mouth as he pressed me into the sofa with his body.

"Shut up, Si," Danny groaned.

CHAPTER 5

An indeterminate but satisfying amount of time later, I was sitting on the edge of the sofa, back in my boxers. Danny was still laid out on the sofa behind me, nude as the day he was born. He had pulled out his vape pen—which he knew I didn't approve of—and was blowing blueish-gray clouds towards the ceiling behind me. I reached up and ran a hand through my disheveled hair and shook my head, amused.

"Blue Raspberry?" I snorted. "What are you? Twelve?"

"It tastes and smells good," he chuckled.

"Smoke cigarettes like a grown up."

"Ah, but then I'd get cancer and you'd have another *ghost* to swindle my mother over."

I ignored the invitation to another fight.

"Those things aren't exactly safe," I said. "They might be causing new diseases that we don't even know about yet."

"Why don't you look in your crystal ball and let me know?"

"I'm a medium and clairvoyant. It doesn't work that way."

"Isn't that convenient?" Danny snorted. "Your powers are only useful when you need them to be."

I turned to glare at him on the sofa behind me as he blew another plume of fog into the air.

"You know what?" I growled.

Danny reached up and put a hand over my mouth, silencing me. I continued to glare at him as he let the hand slide from my mouth to the side of my face. He kept it there, rubbing his thumb tenderly along the apple of my cheek as he smiled up at me.

"I didn't come here to fight, Si," he said. "Don't."

"Stop prodding me," I quipped.

He raised an eyebrow.

"You know what I mean," I said as my cheeks burned.

"All right."

He let his thumb play along my cheekbone a moment longer, then his hand slid down to my neck, over my chest, and back to his side. He took another puff of his vape.

"You'll get that 'popcorn lung' or whatever," I said.

"You told me I'd get lip cancer from the dip in high school," Danny said as he opened his mouth wide. "So far, so good."

"That's because I convinced you to quit before it was too late."

I stood from the sofa. Danny stared up at me, his eyes hungry.

"That's a sight," he said softly.

"I could say the same thing," I replied.

He grinned evilly.

"Oh," I waved him off, "get up. Put your clothes on."

"Suddenly you don't want me here?" Danny grinned and swung his legs over the side of the sofa. "Didn't seem that way a few minutes ago."

"I don't get afterglow," I retorted, "I get annoyed. How long are you going to keep doing this anyway?"

Danny stood and took a puff of his vape right in my face.

"I figure as long as Mom keeps paying you, someone should be getting her money's worth."

I glared at him for a moment.

"I would be offended if that wasn't slightly complimentary. However, for what I charge your Mom, you shouldn't be getting the full-service package."

He laughed. A real laugh, throaty and amused, his head tilting back as he guffawed. Then he was looking at me again.

"I'm going to keep doing this as long as you let me," Danny said softly. "But I still want you to leave my mother alone."

I gave him a sneaky kiss on the lips and stepped away.

"Not going to happen. Get dressed."

Danny slipped the vape pen into the pocket of his jeans on the floor and slipped into his underwear, jeans, and pulled on his t-shirt. He'd gotten his socks and shoes on when he finally spoke again.

"You know," he said, standing before me, "you really will swindle the wrong person one day and end up in jail."

I saw no point in trying to prove I wasn't a fraud to Danny for the millionth time in my life.

"Or I'll end up rich and famous like Victor Grimm with my own T.V. show and theater tour."

Danny gave me an amused shake of his head. I saw no point in further discussions about my abilities or Rhonda Milner and her deceased husband.

"Are you hungry?" I asked.

He gave me a contemplative look.

"I could throw something together," I said. "I don't have anything fancy, but I could make something. Gotta eat anyway, so if you want to join?"

"Nah," Danny replied after a moment. "I really should probably go. I shouldn't have even—"

Before he could finish his thought, headlights poured through the window, diffused by the curtains, and painted the living room walls. With a frown, Danny turned to glance out the window. After a quick peek through the panels of fabric, he turned back to me.

"It's Max," he said.

Slapping a hand to my forehead, I realized how easily I'd been distracted from my evening plans by Danny's appearance on my porch.

"He's bringing a cupboard," I said. "Someone dropped it at his store and he said it'd look nice here."

"How does Max know what would look nice in your house?" Danny squinted at me.

I waved him off.

"Max has a wife and kids," I rolled my eyes. "But you don't own me, either way."

Danny's frown disappeared, but he didn't appear convinced that his competition in Sage Grove was scarce. Not that anyone had to do much to compete with Danny. Our *encounters* were never going to be anything more than a fling. I knew it, Danny knew it, and no one else knew anything about what happened multiple times a week between Danny and I. As far as I was concerned, the two of us were waiting for the lingering boyhood crush from high school to fizzle out so we could both move on.

Someday, I thought to myself as I yanked on my pants, shirt, socks and shoes under Danny's supervision. I headed to the door and swung it open, just as Max was sliding down from the seat of his truck. He waved excitedly, then gestured at the cupboard in the bed, strapped down with rope. From over my shoulder, Danny spoke.

"It does match the walls," he said.

I nodded and stepped out onto the porch. The ghost that had arrived home with me was doing loops around the oak tree further out in the yard, like a hula hoop, floating weightlessly around. I paid him no mind other than to notice his presence, and gave Max a wave.

"Brought a dolly!" Max hollered as he dashed to the back of his truck. "Should be easy!"

I turned to Danny.

"How about I get the full-service from you for once and you go help him?" I muttered.

He said nothing, but ducked around me to dash out into the yard to Max's truck. The two men exchanged pleasantries and general chatter as they worked together to unstrap the cupboard and slide it out of the truck onto the ground. Max had brought the dolly to move the cupboard, as he mentioned, but between the two of them, they were able to lift and carry the cupboard from the yard up to the porch.

With a proud grin, Max slapped the side of the cupboard as he presented it to me on the front porch. As if presenting the cupboard for my approval, and that I would ultimately purchase it, I couldn't help but feel forced into my decision. Now that the cupboard was out of the truck and on my porch, I felt I couldn't really refuse to buy the cupboard. Telling Max and Danny to reload the piece would have seemed cruel. The cost of the cupboard made it seem exceptionally cruel.

"Well," I said, "it does match the walls."

"Kinda shocked you're surprised to see it," Max said.

"You did text me last night. I guess I shouldn't be."

Max frowned. "No. Someone taped a note to it. Thought you knew it was being dropped off at the shop to buy."

"A note?" I asked, glancing at Danny.

"Well, a tag, maybe? Just said 'Silas' on it," Max said with a shrug. "I assumed someone thought you might like it, and, well, I don't know. I guess if you knew it was coming, they'd have dropped it at your place."

I had no reason for why someone would leave a cupboard at Max's shop with my name tagged to it. Of course, like Max, someone might have known the color scheme of my house. In cleaning out old stuff at their house, they might have assumed I'd be interested in some of their old furniture. Who was to say? It was on my porch and I'd offered Max fifty bucks for it.

"As I said, it matches the walls," I replied.

Max's grin widened. He stuffed his hands into the pockets of his baggy work jeans, faded and worn over the years, and looked it up and down lovingly. Obviously, he felt that he had found the perfect match for the piece of furniture that had been unceremoniously dumped at the front of his store. Danny examined the cupboard, squatting and bending to check it out for structural problems or any damage. Unaware that I would pay the agreed upon price regardless of what he found, I left him to his inspection.

"It looks solid," I said, looking the cupboard over.

"Solid wood for sure," Max nodded, his mop of black hair waving with the movement. "Not quite sure what type of wood, though. I can't get the drawers or doors open. Probably been painted shut by the last person. They were probably using it as a show piece instead of storing stuff."

"Aesthetics over function." I nodded.

Danny tugged at the knob on one of the drawers and found it sealed shut. He repeated the action with the left side front door at the top and found himself rejected by the cupboard once more.

Walking around the cupboard, I examined its length, depth, and height. If I was able to strip the paint and get the doors and drawers functional, maybe replace some hinges and tracks, then repaint it a color that wasn't so matchy-matchy with the house, it could be a real find. It would at least be decent storage for dishes or family heirlooms. Even better, it could become the place I stored my most cherished books.

"All right," I said. "It looks like it'll be pretty functional once it's restored. I'll take it."

As if there was ever any doubt.

"Great!" Max clapped his hands together. "Fifty?"

I nodded. "If you help Danny move it inside."

He laughed. "You're the boss, boss!"

Danny stood and gave me a look as though he might decline helping further, simply to get my dander up, but he quickly smiled and shrugged. He fell in with Max and began the task of moving the cupboard into the house. I followed behind them, staying out of the way, glad that both guys were putting up with my laziness. Once we were in the living room, I indicated that they should put the cupboard along the bare wall leading into the kitchen.

"That's good," I said. "Right there. It'll be out of the way until I can get to restoring it."

After the cupboard was in place, I fetched some cash from my wallet while Danny and Max made more guy banter. I couldn't help but feel I'd spent fifty bucks that I could have used for better things, but the cupboard did look nice and solid. Maybe, I thought to myself, if I restore it nicely enough, I could sell it for much more than fifty bucks. Get my money back and put the profit into The Lunch Counter. The possibility lifted my spirits about spending money I didn't really have for something I really didn't need.

"Want me to keep an eye out for a piece for over there?" Max asked, eyeing the corner behind my easy chair. "A bookcase would look great there. Maybe a hutch?"

I waved him off furiously.

"Stop trying to rob me!"

He laughed and stuffed my cash into his pocket as Danny squatted down, examining the cupboard some more.

"All right, all right," Max relented. "But you let me know how it turns out for you. And let me know if you're looking for anything else. That chair is looking a bit worn out."

"Don't insult the easy chair, dude." I warned him playfully. "It has cradled my butt through many-a-television show."

Amused at my statement, Max shook hands with both of us and said his goodbyes. Seconds later, I was shutting the front door as his truck growled down the driveway, away from the house. When I returned to the cupboard, Danny was standing before it, squinting at the paint job.

"Fifty bucks isn't a bad deal," Danny said nonchalantly.

"Yeah."

"If you actually needed the cupboard," he said, grinning, though he didn't turn his head to look at me.

I said nothing.

"You may be a swindler, but you're singlehandedly trying to keep every business in town afloat. Five-dollar milk? Fifty-dollar useless cupboard? The fraud with a heart of gold."

I turned to give him an expressionless stare.

"I'm only kidding."

"I know what you think of me," I said. "And I also know you're here every other night getting in my pants. Maybe you should worry what you think about yourself."

"Si, I—"

"Or," I stopped him, "maybe you should admit to yourself that you don't really think I'm a fraud. You just can't bring yourself to believe something you can't prove."

"Prove it to me, then."

Instead of taking offense, growing red-faced, and blathering angrily at me, Danny simply crossed his arms over his chest and grinned. I stared at him for a moment, peering into his eyes. Finally, I reached out and grabbed his wrist with both hands. He didn't jerk away or look alarmed as I rolled his sleeve up his forearm and lay both hands against the flesh underneath.

Closing my arms, I squeezed his arm and concentrated. I could hear Danny's breath as he watched me stand before him, acting as weird as one could imagine. Finally, after ten seconds, I opened my eyes and found him still staring back at me. I let my hands fall from his arm.

"At lunch you ate a tuna salad sandwich. You ate late because the work load was light and you figured you'd get everything done so you could knock off early."

Danny squinted at me for a moment before responding.

"Touch psychic, eh?" he asked. "You hold onto my arm and that wacky little mind of yours gives you flashes of my past?"

"No," I said. "But I smelled it on your breath when you kissed me. And you never get to your mom's house before I leave. Lucky guess. Maybe I simply pick up clues from people and I am a fraud."

I shrugged. Danny groaned angrily.

"Why do you do this?" He huffed. "I've been calling you a fraud for years! And every time you have a chance to prove it to me, you make a joke out of it! Tell me, Si! Why?"

I shrugged again. "Maybe because I know there's nothing I could tell you that would make you believe me?"

Danny, angry as I'd ever seen him, his face growing red, reached into his back pocket and whipped out his wallet. A second later, I was staring at three twenty-dollar bills. He shoved the money into my chest and held it there.

"There," he said. "The money you spent on this piece of crap and ten to spare. I'm hiring you. Summon my dad. You can't do it for my mom, do it for me."

I shook my head.

"Do it!" Danny insisted. "Right now. Summon my dad. I don't even care that you're swindling my mom to help fund your little charity! Fair enough. She's got the money and it may as well go to a good cause. But prove to me that you're not lying to me. Right now!"

I grabbed his handful of money and pushed it away.

"No."

"No?" Danny barked the question. "Because you can't and you really are a fraud, or you want to be cruel? Maybe you're dragging things out with Mom to keep reeling in the dough you need for The Lunch Counter. Fine. I won't tell her. But I need to know. Right now."

"Just no," I said, simply.

"Why?" Danny was no longer angry.

He was pleading. The look in his eyes having changed from the accusatory look of someone encountering a fraud to that of a wounded boy who desperately wanted proof his father was safe in the afterlife nearly had me losing my resolve.

"Ghosts can't come in my house anyway," I said, then continued before he could suggest alternative locations. "And talking to your dad won't bring you the closure you think it will."

"But—"

"It never does, Danny," I shook my head slowly at him. "I've done this enough to know that there's no such thing as closure."

"What does that even mean?" Danny pleaded, though the anger was seeping back into his voice as he loomed before me.

"People find out grandpa really was murdered. Then they become obsessed with finding the murderer, even though it happened fifty years ago. People find out their best friend did kill themselves and wonder if they could have said or done something differently. Reached out more often. Gotten them help. They find out that Mom hid the jewels at a relative's house to keep them from getting them and they begin to question their entire relationship with Mom before she died. Knowing what goes on over there on the other side only brings up more questions. Sometimes it's best to let the dead rest."

Danny was glowering at me.

"One day, hopefully far in the future, you can ask him all your questions yourself," I said quietly. "I promise you it's highly possible."

"But you won't summon him and ask him one question, right now, to prove I'm not sleeping with a fraud who's swindling my mother?"

I shook my head, lowering my eyes to look at the floor. Danny breathed out slowly, heatedly, and glowered down at me a moment longer. Then, he stepped around me and headed to the front door. I waited for the inevitable opening of the door, the slamming, the sound of angry footsteps out to his truck. Instead, Danny suddenly stopped behind me.

"You know what?" he asked angrily. "Here's the money."

His hand was suddenly in my hip pocket, stuffing the twenties into it.

"You're going to need it," he said, cryptically.

"Screw this cupboard," Danny growled.

I looked up to see Danny stomping towards the cupboard and I immediately realized what he had in mind. My head whipped around to the cupboard, mourning its impending destruction. However, in those few moments I had to stare at it, dreading the destruction that was to come, my eyes landed on the weird raised numbs at the corners of all of the doors and drawers. Something at the corner of each had been painted over when the cupboard had been redone.

Danny was already swinging his fist at the top cupboard door when I realized what I had spotted. Attempting to put myself between Danny and the cupboard was an exercise in futility. My brain had been too slow for me to stop the inevitable. Opening my mouth to shout at Danny to stop, I watched in terror as his fist seemed to fly through the air in slow motion towards the top doors of the cabinet.

"*STOOOOOOOP!*" I heard myself scream as Danny's fist connected with the wood.

Desperately, in the split second I had to pray, I hoped that Danny's fist would be no match for the solid wood. Unfortunately, a lifetime of sports and construction work had given Danny the strength he needed to achieve his goal in one try. As his fist went solidly through the right door of the cabinet, my eyes went wide. All time seemed to stop as I stared at his fist sticking through the splintered wood of the cabinet. Danny, red-faced and huffing, was readying to pull his fist back to deliver a blow to the other door.

Before he could extract his arm from the interior of the cabinet, the shimmery white fog peeked out from the hole his arm had created. Staring into the eyes of the ghost in the cupboard, I started to scream again. However, before my mouth could open, the ghost, in a wintry gust of cold air, zipped out of the cupboard, whirled around Danny, and disappeared around the wall into the kitchen.

Danny's arm came out of the cupboard and he stumbled backwards, landing in a heap on the floor. With wide eyes, I looked down at the tangle of arms and legs on the floor before me. My eyes darted from the wrecked cupboard door, towards the kitchen, then down at Danny, over and over again.

On the floor, Danny shivered.

"What in the heck was that?" Danny asked, his face nearly as pale as the ghost that now had unfettered access to my home.

CHAPTER 6

"A ghost?" Danny asked. "In the cupboard?"

Picking at the nub in the lower right-hand corner below the door Danny had smashed with his fist, I desperately peel away the newer paint.

"Yes."

"Someone...trapped a ghost in a cupboard and now the ghost is loose in your house?" Danny asked, incredulous.

"Don't give me that nonbeliever stuff," I grumbled as I picked at the paint furiously. "I saw your face. You felt it."

Danny began babbling incoherently behind me as my fingernail finally found purchase and peeled back the layer of bumpy green paint. I palmed the sliver of paint and squatted down to look at the nub of metal it had been covering.

The shiny silver piece flickered in the overhead living room light and my stomach dropped. I glanced at the other corners of the doors and drawers and knew there was no point in investigating those nubs. They were all surely silver. The ghost that was now God knows where in my house had been trapped in the cupboard. And now it was my problem.

Sighing, I rose to a standing position.

"All I felt was cold air, Si!" Danny demanded. "I didn't see any ghost. This is ridiculous. If you want to prove to me that you can communicate with ghosts, this is—"

"Get out," I said softly.

"Wha-what?"

"Go home, Danny," I said as I turned to him. "Get out. I have bigger problems right now than your doubts."

"I...I mean...we...this is..."

"Yeah, yeah," I said, pushing him towards the door. "I don't care. Go home. I can't deal with you and this right now. Get."

Danny stammered protestations that ranged from angry to confused to scared as I hustled him out of the house. He was still blathering when I slammed and locked the front door in his face. I leaned back against the door, listening to him stammer his thoughts out on the front porch through the door for several minutes before he finally stopped. A few moments later, I heard footsteps on the porch, crunching in the yard, and then the sound of his truck door.

A moment later, I heard the truck start up and drive off. I turned and stood on tiptoes to look out at the yard. His truck was headed off down the driveway. When my eyes shifted over to my car, Chester was standing by the hood. He smiled, black ooze dripping from the corner of his mouth, as he waved excitedly at me. I did my best to return his smile before giving him a quick wave and pushing away from the door.

Standing in the middle of the living room, I opened my hand and looked down at the piece of paint it held. Green and bumpy, like the walls of my house, I could immediately tell it had been infused with sage ash. Why I hadn't noticed it when Max had brought the cupboard to the house, I had no idea. However, it quickly dawned on me that I had been distracted when Max arrived with the cupboard.

Danny.

I had been so focused on not making a fuss about him while Max was around—for fear that Max would figure out what was going on between us. Furthermore, I hadn't wanted Danny to say anything about me being a fraud around Max. Also, it had been dark out on the front porch. I hadn't gotten a good look at it, not really, before the guys had brought it in the house. Once inside, I wasn't really worried about the cupboard anymore because Danny had distracted me once again.

If he had left before smashing the cupboard, and I'd had time to look it over before opening it, I would have known better. I would have pushed it right back out on the porch before attempting to pry it open to reveal the secrets within. The ghost would have been let out in the yard instead of my home. Now…I had decisions to make. Decisions I rarely had to make anymore that I never enjoyed.

Of course, there was one other glaring problem that should have been my first thought. Who had trapped a ghost in a cupboard? Not only that, *how* had they known how to trap a ghost at all? It wasn't everyday knowledge at all that ghosts existed, that they could be trapped, or how they could be trapped. Your average human has no reason to even be concerned with ghosts, let alone how to deal with them.

Obviously, if you ask around, you'll find at least a handful of people who claim they've had a ghostly encounter. An old house they lived in where they felt cold chills or heard odd noises in the night. People who woke up to weird shadows or a sinking feeling in the bed next to them. People who briefly saw an apparition floating down the hall or watching them from the foot of their bed. Their knowledge rarely went beyond these sightings.

People move house and the hauntings stop. They have a priest bless a house and the ghost might move on, not wanting to deal with the uncomfortable feeling of a blessed house. Victims of a haunting may convince themselves they're simply making things up and mentally block the ghosts without knowing they're actively doing it.

More esoteric knowledge—the silver and sage, how to effectively deal with a haunting—is not common. Whoever had painted the cupboard, trapped the ghost, and then set the cupboard outside Max's shop, had more than a base level working knowledge of ghosts. In a town like Sage Grove, I knew of only one person.

Silas Erie.

Me.

And I hadn't trapped a ghost or painted a cupboard. I certainly hadn't put forth the effort of lugging a heavy piece of furniture over to Max's shop and left it on his front door. So, contemplating how the ghost had ended up in the cupboard, and how the cupboard ended up in my possession, and the ghost ended up in my house was pointless. Dealing with the immediate problem was the only action that seemed reasonable.

Shaking my head clear of all the pointless theories and conspiracies, I marched away from the cupboard and into the kitchen. I stood in the doorway to the kitchen and let my eyes pan over its contents. Nothing seemed out of place, no cabinet doors slightly ajar, nothing knocked over. I certainly didn't find a ghost hiding under the table, cowering with fear, when I walked over and squatted down to check.

So, I moved to the hallway. The hall bathroom. The bedrooms. Back to the living room.

No ghost was found hiding behind the shower curtain. Or a closet. Under the beds. Hiding in a different cupboard or hidey-hole. It had simply disappeared. However, the gnawing at my gut was only growing.

An important fact to know about ghost-proofing a house so that ghosts can't get in is that once one gets out, it's difficult to make them leave on their own. A ghost can be trapped inside a house as easily as it can be trapped outside. The silver around the doors, windows, and other entry points in my house, along with the sage ash imbued paint, meant that the ghost that had escaped the cupboard, would never be able to escape my house. Even if it wanted to do it.

Not without assistance.

"Hey," I said, "where are you? I know you're in here somewhere."

Standing in the middle of the living room and talking to thin air produced no results. Another fun fact about ghosts—unless you actually know a ghost's name, it cannot be summoned by force. At least, not specifically. A medium, such as myself, can always reach out to the spirit realm and come up with any number of ghosts. However, if I wanted to summon a particular ghost, I needed to know their name. Otherwise, unless they heard the random call to the spirit realm and chose to check it out, they might ignore the call.

A name holds power.

Theoretically, with enough psychic power, and a name, a trained medium could control a ghost. Get it to do the medium's bidding. The implication of such a thing is terrifying, if you think about it. The government could employ a medium and their army of ghostly spies. A medium could use ghosts to collect blackmail material. The possibilities are endless. It's another good reason to ghost proof your house. If no ghosts can get in or out, your home is a safe space from any medium who has chosen to use their powers for not so good things.

I'd never attempted to control a ghost in my entire life. The descent into madness and criminal malevolence on the path to power and money is more slippery than a banana peel on a marble floor. One minute you're a medium simply wanting to increase your income potential, the next you're trading government secrets with Russia and nukes are flying overhead.

Maybe that's an exaggeration, but the truth remains.

Ghosts are not meant to be used for evil.

"What's your name?" I asked. "Mine is Silas. Silas Erie. Talk to me."

I turned slowly in the living room, waiting for any sign of the ghost. Not so much as a peek of an eye from under a piece of furniture or, as trite as it might be, a "boo." I made another round through the house, still finding nothing, before the time on my phone screen caught my attention. It was nearing nine o'clock, and there was still work to be done before bedtime.

Though it made me feel uneasy after years of having a spook-free home, I knew I had no choice but to ignore the present ghost issue. I breezed through the kitchen and hurriedly made a plate with sandwich fixings from the fridge, along with a healthy pile of chips alongside it. I took my plate down the hall and pushed open the doorway at the end.

Inside, I took found myself in the moonlight pouring through the glass ceiling and walls of the hexagonal room. A couple of ghosts were floating lazily, listlessly, through the room, their dull eyes focused on nothing. The atrium was the only room of the house that ghosts could enter—and for good reason. It was where I did all of my internet requests for help contacting dead loved ones.

The atrium was a space to do my spirit work in a more controlled, more comfortable environment, safe from too many prying eyes. It also gave me a way to work in my house while also keeping any of the ghosts I summoned from actually entering the spaces where I lived my day-to-day life.

Vines from ivy plants climbed the trellises in the corners, winding their way up the windows. Potted spider plants reached towards the ceiling with their spiky leaves. A four-foot diameter round table sat in the center of the terra cotta tiled floor. Two chairs, across from each other, were pushed under the table. My laptop, its charging cord strung from the charging port in the side of the computer to the plug ten feet away in the wall, was closed, waiting on me. Only moonlight pouring through the glass illuminated the room, casting it in a midnight blue color.

With a sigh, I set my plate of food on the table next to the laptop and pulled the chair out. The feet of the chair scratched against the rough tile before I finally fell into the seat. Simultaneously shoving a handful of chips into my mouth and opening the laptop, it was time to work. Once the laptop was open and I'd typed in my passcode, I went about lighting the single pillar candle that sat at the center of the table. About as big around as my thigh and nearly eight inches tall, the white candle had six wicks to light.

Though too much light made me feel exposed, since anyone who walked onto my property would be able to see inside the room, lighting all of the candle's wicks was necessary. So large was the candle that if all of the wicks didn't burn at once, the candle would burn unevenly. So, once I was cast in the warm golden glow of, virtually, six candles burning a mere foot away, I opened the email app on my professional website.

In the blue glow of the laptop screen and the yellow glow of the candle, I sorted through the emails waiting on me. There were plenty of requests for help, but I always focused on prepaid requests. Money gets any request put to the front of the line. Potential clients wanting to ask questions first would have to wait until I'd done the jobs for which I'd already been paid. Fortunately, a little programming from a tech buddy had helped me create a system that sorted my email by paid and unpaid. I opened the first one that was tagged as paid.

Hello, Mr. Erie. My father passed away fifteen days ago, and—

Another person who had a deceased relative with a missing will. I clicked on another email indicated as paid.

Hi, Silas! I wanted to know if you could contact my cousin and ask her what her favorite animal was. I ask because—

I don't need your explanation, I thought to myself. You are testing if I'm for real before you hire me for another job. I rolled my eyes and opened yet another email.

Mr. Erie. I'm writing to you because my mother's dying words were—

Someone who wanted clarification about a dying family member's last thought. Easy enough.

At least a dozen other emails were listed in the paid folder. It was a great day for requests. I easily had a thousand dollars of prepaid requests sitting in my email folder.

Time to get to work. I reached out for another chip, finding that side of the plate was empty. I'd scarfed them all down while checking out emails. So, I grabbed the sandwich and sat back in the chair. Taking a healthy bite of the corner of the ham and cheese, I stared at the candle on the table for a moment, trying to clear my mind of other worries. The two ghosts that had been in the atrium when I'd entered were now in different corners, bobbing above the ground lazily, staring with blank eyes at me.

I opened the first email I'd looked at for a second time. I cleared my throat and spoke loudly and clearly.

"Scooter Dubois!"

I rolled my eyes at the name, hoping the client had provided the man's government name instead of a nickname.

"I'm Silas Erie, medium, lifeline to the dead, communicator with souls. I have a question from your son. Unfinished business you have on this earth. I summon you!"

I took another large bite of my sandwich and chewed quietly as I stared at the candle on the table. A minute ticked by. Then another. The floating ghosts in the corners continued to mind their business. As I was taking another bite of my sandwich, a third ghosts suddenly burst through the glass wall of the atrium, headed directly for the open door into the house. When it hit the invisible wall created by the pieces of silver in the corners of the door, it bounced back and spun, twirling violently in the air.

I waited patiently, gnawing at my sandwich as the ghost finished twirling. When it came to a stop, facing away from me, I put the leftover half of my sandwich on the plate. I wiped my hands on the knees of my jeans and sat up.

"Were you Scooter Dubois in life?" I asked.

The ghost, startled since it hadn't noticed me yet, spun around to face me. Hazy and diaphanous, the floating ghost looked down at me, the door behind it clearly visible through its body. When it merely stared at me, unspeaking, I began to worry that Scooter Dubois was Screamer—a lost cause. A client that would be refunded, no matter how much it bothered me.

"Can you speak?" I asked. "Were you Scooter Dubois?"

The ghost, suddenly finding its voice, was offended.

"*I* am *Scooter Dubois!*"

"Were," I said, glancing at my laptop. "You died fifteen days ago in your bed at home. Are you aware of that yet?"

Scooter Dubois didn't answer, but he didn't look shocked. Which was good. Walking ghosts through the whole alive-dead thing was always a chore. I wasn't a trained therapist, simply a medium. I never enjoyed having to walk ghosts through the grief process, simply because it took so much out of me emotionally as well. Time was also an issue. I had too many ghosts to summon before bed would get my attention.

"*Yeeeeeees,*" Scooter moaned. "*I am aware. I was* Scooter Dubois."

Good, I thought. A ghost who catches on quickly.

"Okay," I replied with a nod before looking at the email details once more. "Your son, uh, Darrell, wants to know where you put your will. Apparently, your arrangements with it and its placement elude him."

Before I could blink, the ghost was towering over the table, growling in my face. My hair blew back as the anger radiated off Scooter Dubois's now terrifying glowing form. His mouth snapped open like a gator's maw, an impossible number of teeth shining in his mouth, the back of his throat like a tunnel into an abyss. Fortunately, this was not my first rodeo. I didn't so much as blink at the sudden development.

"*Darrell is no son of mine! Greedy! Vile! Wicked, wicked boy! He will not receive one penny from me! I should have drowned him at birth! I should have—*"

"Great," I said, blandly. "Will any of what you just said be a surprise to him, or will he be expecting it?"

Scooter Dubois, startled back into his former ghostly form, was floating across the table from me once again. I started to type, waiting for a response. When Scooter remained silent, I looked over at him.

"I'm on the clock, Scooter," I said. "I need to know what to tell him. Do you want me to tell him you refuse to say where your will is? Do you want to send a specific message to prove you have been summoned? I don't do curse words or insults or relay information involving crimes committed or you want committed, and I won't tell him anything that will ruin his life unless it has to do with the will—but I can give him the gist of an abusive message if you like since he did ask about the will."

Not knowing what to make of me, Scooter looked down at the ground for a moment. Finally, as my fingertips hovered over the laptop, he lifted his head and looked me in the face.

"*Tell him he was never and is not now or ever a son of mine*," Scooter's ghostly wail echoed in my ears as I began to type. "*Tell him his brother, Cecil, is my sole benefactor. It is outlined in my will—which my lawyer possesses. He will contact Cecil in the timeframe I have provided to my lawyer. On Cecil's eighteenth birthday.*"

"Sounds good," I said. "I can do that. Will he feel that this message is truly from you, or would you like to include a response that lets him know I have truly contacted you?"

Scooter thought on this.

"*Tell him that mohawk he had in eighth grade was a dumbass decision.*"

I looked up at him to grin.

"Is that why he's cut out of the will?" I asked, mostly joking.

"*He had an affair with his stepmother.*"

Blinking, I stared at Scooter for several moments. Finally, I breathed in deeply through my nose.

"Mr. Dubois, if this was any other night, I'd grab a beer and invite you to have a seat," I chuckled. "However, I have a busy night ahead of me. Unless there is anything else you would care to say to Darrell, I have to move along to other ghosts."

Saying nothing, Scooter Dubois's ghostly form nodded its head, then slowly drifted through the table, through me, and back out of the atrium once more, its head held high. I always hated the icy cold hand of death from ghosts as they passed through me, but there was no way to stop ghosts from doing it if they so wished. Instead, I turned back to my laptop, typed out an abridged version of events to Darrell, and sent off the email. Of course, I always include a message to clients that I'm always available for future services, but I felt I'd never hear from Darrell Dubois ever again.

Unless it was to request a refund. Which he wouldn't get.

I grabbed my sandwich and moved on to the next email. It was going to be a long night.

CHAPTER 7

That night, I dreamt of the first ghostly encounter I'd ever had in my life. My mother and I were in the living room; it was just the two of us by the time I was thirteen. Dad, grandmas, grandpas, everyone was gone then. My older sister had already moved on, out of state, to live with her new husband and finish college. So, time couldn't have presented itself better.

My dream wasn't quite truthful, since, even awake, I could never recall all of the details of that day. Obviously, many details had been filled in by my sleeping brain to help the dream make sense. I was sitting on the sofa, my mother next to me, so close our knees tapped each other if we moved at all. We were staring down at the large wooden box on the coffee table before us.

What is it? I'd asked excitedly.

After a long, tense moment, which made no sense to me, my mother finally breathed out her response.

A test.

Excitedly, I stared at the wooden box with the weird paint and the silver inlays at every single corner. At thirteen, I was a studious young man who loved school and devoured any book I could get my hands on. A test? What fun!

I can't say I'm not proud of that fact as an adult, but's also a piece of personal lore that makes me uncomfortable to admit to others to this day.

What kind of test? Is it a puzzle?

No. Not a puzzle. A…sight and hearing test.

Confused by my mother's words, I stared more intensely at the box. What was I supposed to be hearing and seeing?

When I open this box, my mother said, *tell me what you see, Silas. What you hear. Okay?*

Nodding excitedly, I was practically gnashing my teeth, waiting for the test.

My mother took a deep breath, patted my knee, and reached for the lid of the box. As she slid it back, I could feel my heart thundering in my chest, a single bead of sweat dribbling over my temple to the apple of my cheek. And then the lid was off.

And my life changed forever.

It wasn't until a handful of years later, when my mother was bedridden, holding on to her quickly ending life, that I found out my sister had also taken The Test.

She had failed; I had passed.

And I was the last of our bloodline at the time, causing me to vow, in that moment, sitting over my mother's soon-to-be deathbed, that I would never have to give The Test to a child.

Regardless of nightmares, life goes on every morning, whether one likes it or not. My morning after summoning so many ghosts, then dreaming about my first encounter with a ghost, proved to be trying. Having my head in the wrong space meant I nearly punched myself in the face brushing my teeth, I could barely get my hair brushed and styled, I almost slipped in the shower, and getting dressed was nearly impossible.

By the time I got into my car and headed into town, I knew exactly where I was headed. However, I first stopped at the Gas & Go for an energy drink. Caleb was on duty again, the blinds at the front of the store shut tightly to the morning sun. He rang me up for the giant can and ducked back, blinking his eyes at the sun that slivered in the front door when I left.

77

I had to feel bad for the guy. The Gas & Go faced easterly and was unobstructed by other buildings from the rising sun. Anyone working the morning shift could easily spend the day blinded by the sun pouring through the giant plate glass windows. Fortunately, the blinds on the windows made working morning shifts easier.

As I left the gas station, I popped the top of the can and began to chug as I walked down to Shop-A-Teria. Max Nguyen was pulling up in his truck and parking outside of the grocery store when I walked up. He waved from the interior of his truck, shut it off, and hopped out quickly upon seeing me. I gave him a head nod as I approached, then slammed another quarter of the can of energy.

"Mornin'," Max announced before leaning back into his truck for his phone. He slipped it into his back jeans pocket before closing the door and turning to me again. "Don't tell me you want to return that cabinet."

I chuckled nervously. Unfortunately, I didn't think Max would take the cupboard back after Danny's alterations.

"I've already made some changes so there'd be no point in trying," I said.

"Good!" Max said, leaning back against his truck as he spoke to me. "What can I do you for then, Si?"

I took another slug of my drink.

"Any idea who left it outside the Shop-A-Teria?" I asked. "I have some questions for the previous owner."

Good old Max—he didn't so much as raise an eyebrow of suspicion. The new owner of a cupboard having questions to pose to the previous owner was completely reasonable. Why wouldn't the new owner have questions? Perfectly understandable that I'd want to ask questions about the unique piece of furniture.

"You know how it is, Si," Max said. "Folks know I have that room off the side there for selling used home goods. Hardly anyone says anything when they drop stuff off. They just dump it near the entry there, where the elements can't easily get to it, and leave."

I sagged, but I understood.

"I can call around," Max offered. "I'm sure, given enough time, I could find the owner, if it's that important to you."

"No," I said, waving him off, though I really wanted to know, "don't go to all that trouble. Calling all over town is just as easy for me as it is for you."

Max shrugged. "Well, if you change your mind, let me know. I'll do what I can."

"Thanks, Max," I said.

With a wave and a smile, he left me beside his truck and headed up to the automatic glass door at the front of the small grocery store. Under the shade of the awning, his keys jingled as he unlocked the door and reached up to the turn the switch to "automatic." As he stepped through the door, he shot me another smile and then headed off to start his day.

I finished my energy drink as I took in the building. Like many of the other buildings on the main thoroughfare, the two-story red brick building was a landmark with historical significance. Presently, the renovated bottom floor housed a small grocery store and the second floor stood vacant. No one cared about the building, save the man who ran his business out of it.

The ten-by-ten stone smokehouse that had been built to the side of the building decades ago was now a secondhand homewares and furniture store. All of these facts were known to everyone in town. Anyone could have set the cupboard outside at night for Max to find when he came into work in the morning.

No one lived downtown proper anymore. Not really. And the only all-night business was the Gas & Go and the Wash-A-Teria. The laundromat wasn't staffed at night, solely self-serve. So, whoever was working overnight at the gas station was my best bet if I was to look for witnesses. It was possible that someone doing late-night laundry might have also witnessed the cupboard's drop off.

If Sal had listened to me, she had moved the unhoused folks into Doc Stephens' old officer building the previous night. That's the information I'd passed along to her, anyway. Sal and I worked together to make sure that during the cold months, the unhoused from her camp knew which abandoned buildings were safe to sleep in overnight.

Sage Grove had no real police force, but county officers would do a nightly drive through town, to make sure everything looked safe and sound. Once every other week, they'd do a more thorough check of town, checking out abandoned buildings, stopping and checking with residents to make sure everything was copasetic. When they came to check out buildings, Caleb would watch out for them. He'd pass long which buildings had been checked, and I'd pass that along to Sal. They never checked the same building in the same week, so once a building had been checked, it was a safe sleeping spot for the unhoused folks for at least a handful of nights.

Before Doc Stephens' office building, Sal had all of the folks from the camp sleeping in an abandoned house on the outskirts of town. However, it had a mold problem and it was so dilapidated that sleeping outside wouldn't have been much different. None of them would have seen the cupboard dropped off since they were nowhere near town center.

Basically, as I destroyed my kidneys with chemicals and caffeine outside the grocery store, I could conclude that finding the previous owner of the cupboard would be incredibly difficult. Unless Caleb had seen something, I was going to have to start asking around. Even though Sage Grove presently had less than a thousand residents—*and dwindling*—asking around could take forever unless I got lucky.

I walked back to Gas & Go and my car with an empty can and clearer thoughts. Where the cupboard had come from didn't matter in the grand scheme of things. It wouldn't help me get the ghost out of my house any quicker. But someone had put my name on the cupboard, which was concerning.

Like most sane people with the knowledge, experience, and know-how, they had a ghost and they wanted to get rid of it. Obviously, everything else was incidental. My worrying about the details of where, why, and how the ghost had ended up in the cupboard didn't matter. Especially since those details would be nearly impossible to acquire.

Get rid of the ghost before it gets comfortable.

That would be my goal.

I tossed the empty energy drink into the back floorboard of my car and hopped into the driver's seat. Getting to The Lunch Counter to start prepping for the meal of the day would take my mind off of things. However, when I rounded the corner to drive down to the diner, the mob waiting outside told me my day wasn't going to get easier.

CHAPTER 8

"It's not fair, Silas!" Sal was shaking a paper in my face as I climbed out of my car. "Look at this!"

Four of the homeless folks, including Gary, were with her, waiting to talk to me. Ginny was over by the front door of the diner, trying to get it unlocked, shooting me an apologetic look. Obviously, she'd been attacked by the crowd first, seen me coming, and turned their attention to me. Upon being distracted by my arrival, she'd slipped away.

That's a true friend for you.

"What's not fair?" I grunted, doing my best to wiggle out of the car with five people pressing in against me. "What's got you all riled up so early in the morning?"

"This!" Sal barked, shaking the paper in her hand. "I am fit to be tied, Silas! Fit to be tied! They can't do this to us! To the town! How come they are—"

I grabbed the paper out of Sal's hand, silencing her with a crooked frown. My message had been made clear—I had to know what she was talking about to respond. Waving a paper in my face wasn't going to help any. Glancing over my shoulder, I'd found that Ginny had managed to slip into the diner, avoiding any further outbursts from the group of folks.

"What is this?" I asked, speaking mostly to myself, as I examined the paper Sal had been holding.

Out of the corner of my eye, I noticed Gary eyeing the front door of the shop. If he went inside and started staring at Ginny,

I'd have another screaming Banshee. I looked up from the paper I hadn't even started to read yet, and locked eyes with Gary.

"It's burgers and fries today, Gary," I said. "Saturday, remember?"

Gary, slightly startled, jerked, but then nodded, and stepped away from the diner's front door. Rejoining our little mix of folks in his own way, Gary stood behind his friends, staring down at his feet as I put my attention back on the paper. After a quick glance, I looked up at Sal and huffed.

"It's the same thing the county police have been posting for months," I said. "Why are you so out of sorts?"

"Look at it, Si!" One of the other folks demanded, jabbing their finger at the paper. "They're trying to run us out of here!"

The person who had spoken up, I believed, was the one they called "Suzie-Q" down at the camp. I wasn't certain if the middle-aged woman in flannels, secondhand bib overalls, boots, and a puffer jacket looked much like the name. However, her brown curls kind of made the whole thing make sense. Sometimes a single physical attribute can explain an entire, seemingly, mismatched nickname.

"It's the same notice that they've been putting on all the abandoned buildings," I said, calmly. "If they find people squatting, they'll arrest them, board up the buildings better, blah blah blah. It's just an attempt to scare you all into staying down by the river."

"Well," Sal spoke up, "it's working! I can't be getting arrested, Si! All I have left is my freedom."

I did my best to give her a sympathetic look.

"Look," I said, "you all know county is not going to spend time, money, and officers, coming around here often enough to catch you all squatting at night. Just keep doing what you've been doing. Stay outside in the day unless it's unavoidable, and take shelter at night."

"How long will that work?" A voice to my side asked. "How long before they start tearing down buildings to keep us from being able to live?"

The question wasn't a bad one. For my entire life, I'd known that any government, local or otherwise, existed to make people's lives harder—especially those they deemed lesser than. The homeless population of Sage Grove was literally hurting no one using abandoned buildings at night to stay out of the elements and stay safe. Stapling notices to the buildings that they'd be arrested, the buildings would be sealed better—or even destroyed—was nothing more than cruelty.

Fortunately, our local government didn't really have the time or resources to carry through with their threats. They might be able to find an officer or two to swing by in the middle of the night and check things out, maybe nail a few windows and doors shut, but that was it. The unhoused population had to deal with the indignity of the notices, but they weren't going to lose their squatting places anytime soon.

"You can't tell us this isn't a real threat, Silas!" Ronny-Boy spoke up. He was shifting nervously next to me, pulling at the ripped cuffs of his long-sleeve shirt. "We all saw what they did with The Eternity!"

I rolled my eyes. The Eternity Inn had been a point of contention in the community for months.

"The county didn't seal it up," I said to Ronny-Boy. "The Milners did that before Harlan died. You know how they are. The thought of anyone using one of their properties without paying was too much for them."

The group around me couldn't help but chuckle. The Milners had their fingers in tons of businesses and ventures.

They were capitalists through and through. The Eternity Inn had been purchased by the family in the 30s and been in the family ever since. However, in the last few decades, with the loss of population and commerce in Sage Grove, the Inn had closed. Shortly before Harlan's death, the family had the place sealed up—and it would probably stay that way now that Harlan was dead. Rumors swirled that Rhonda was selling off many of the businesses and properties owned by the Milner Corporation.

"If the corporation can't sell it, they'll end up bulldozing it and giving the land back to the city," I explained. "It's a business decision. Nothing to do with y'all."

"Are you sure?" Sal spoke up for the group. "Winter will be here before long. What'll happen if they seal up every place in town? Or worse, tear 'em all down? We'll have nowhere to stay warm."

I stood before the small group of representatives from the camp and looked them all in the eyes, one by one.

"I will make sure you have somewhere to sleep at night in winter." I made my vow. "Even if you're sleeping in The Lunch Counter at night, we'll figure something out. All right? Do you all feel better now?"

I was met with four smiles and one crooked attempt from Gary. Finally, I was able to usher the group away from the diner, allowing me to go about my day as normal. Sal muttered a quick apology as she led everyone back to camp, also letting me know she'd be back later to pick up lunch for everyone. Gary lingered behind the pack, glancing over his shoulder at me numerous times as they all walked away.

Frowning, I couldn't help but feel that Gary wanted to speak to me, but didn't know how. In fact, I wasn't sure Gary was even capable of speaking anymore. I hadn't heard a word come from his mouth in months. When he finally stopped looking back at me and continued on with the rest of the group, I pushed him from my mind. If the man wanted to speak with me—or communicate in some way—he knew where to find me.

Giving the notice from the county that I held in my hand another look, I stuffed it in the trashcan by the front door of The Lunch Counter. Upon entering the diner, I caught the scent of onions being prepped for the day. Fortunately, Ginny was working on the onions in the back of the diner, so my eyes didn't immediately start watering. I slipped out of my coat and went to wash my hands before joining Ginny at the back of the diner.

"It's every day with them, Si," Ginny said as soon as I stepped into the prep area. "Sal is getting them riled up day after day. Before you know it, they'll be running wild through town, setting stuff on fire out of panic."

I couldn't help but chuckle, but Ginny's characterization of Sal and the other homeless folks in town didn't sit right with me.

"They're people," I said. "Not wild animals."

"People *are* wild animals," Ginny said. "This has nothing to do with the fact that they're homeless. It's the fact that humans can be manipulated so easily into panic and disorder. Sal isn't helping them at all, jumping to crazy panics every time the county posts a stupid notice on a dilapidated building."

"Fair," I said.

"She knows as well as we do the county is going to keep posting those form letters every now and then to keep them on their toes," Ginny continued as she chopped an onion. "But they're never going to follow through with the threats. Why would they waste money on the tools, supplies, and manpower, dealing with buildings that have been sitting vacant for years in Sage Grove?"

I laughed. Ginny explained the situation much better than I had. She should have talked to Sal and her group for me.

"You know that," I said. "I know that. Sal and the rest of the camp group can't help but worry. When you have no home, no real income, have food insecurity…it's hard not to panic every time the county does something cruel like that."

"I guess," Ginny said. "I relent, okay?"

We both chuckled as we worked.

"However, you have to admit, you do so much for them and all they do is show up with problems and complaints," Ginny said. "When are you going to say enough is enough and Victor Grimm this thing?"

She gestured vaguely at my head with her chef's knife before she went back to chopping onions.

"*Victor Grimm this thing?*" I repeated.

"You know," Ginny nodded, not looking up at me. "Sell out. Talk to spirits on T.V. for religious nuts looking for closure from grandma and whatnot? Help the police solve missing persons cases. Do TikToks. Have a merch store. That kind of thing."

"I'm not certain everything you just said is even English," I replied. "I don't get involved with religious nuts, social media trends, or merchandise. And I don't get involved in crimes."

"Well," Ginny said, "Victor does. Though I can't say that I've heard of him *actually* helping to solve one. I'm not certain he's very good at summoning spirits."

He's a charlatan, I thought to myself. An attractive man made up a persona, donned the regalia he thought would sell the vibe, and learned to con people. *He can't actually speak to spirits.*

"Some of us have a moral code," I said instead of letting all my thoughts leak out of my mouth.

"What kind of moral code keeps you from helping the police solve murders?" Ginny cackled. "Isn't that the complete opposite of morality."

"Okay," I said. "Follow me here, all right?"

I set the bag of potatoes I had grabbed from the pantry by the prep sink and turned to Ginny. She set the knife down and turned to face me, her arms going across her chest.

"You die today," I said. "Who are you mad at?"

"Let me get my list," Ginny said with a snort.

"If you could peg your death on one of them, knowing there's no real consequence for you, would you do it?"

"Why would a ghost do that?"

"Why *wouldn't* a ghost do that?" I asked. "They're just the spirit-slash-personality of the person they were in life. They're the same as they always were, except floating around, invisible to most, without any substance. They can be rude, vindictive, cruel—also nice and moral and stuff—but there are no more consequences for their actions like when they were human and could go to prison. If they pin a murder on someone for giggles, it won't affect them. So...how can you trust a ghost to tell the truth?"

Ginny thought about this, then her face brightened.

"What about Heaven and Hell?" she asked. "Wouldn't the fear of eternal damnation or the promise of life in eternal bliss help them be moral?"

I flattened her with a frown.

"If Heaven and Hell exist, why are so many of these things still floating around?" I asked. "I'm sorry, my friend, but if Heaven or Hell exist, I've yet to see proof of it. Sometimes, when I pass on a message for a ghost, they seem to go…somewhere? They *move on* or whatever, but I have no idea what that means. Regardless, how can you trust a ghost?"

"Well, couldn't you give the cops the information the ghost gave you and that'll set them on the right path?" Ginny asked. "Give them something to chase down?"

"I suppose," I said. "But, one, you have to get the cops to believe you can talk to ghosts. Two, you have to believe ghosts always tell the truth. Three, you have to understand that even ghosts can be wrong when they're not necessarily being deceitful. And lastly, you could easily give cops bad information that takes them off the right track and stalls or ruins their investigation. Ethically and morally, I do not get involved with crimes. Period."

"Fine!" Ginny threw her hands up comically with a huge grin. "Don't help the cops! I get it! Don't summon spirits on national T.V. or have branded merchandise. Don't wear shirts that show your pecs or tight pants that—"

"Stop it." I warned her.

Ginny cackled.

"Do what feels best to you, Si," Ginny said. "That way, when you become a ghost, you can know you were ethically and morally superior and float around waiting for the promise of a heaven that never existed."

She turned back to the prep table, grabbed her knife, and started chopping onions once more, proud of herself.

"Hey," I said, "I have to live—and unlive—with myself for eternity. It's not just Heaven that can be a reward."

She gave me a quick wink and went back to the onions. I bent down to grab the sack of potatoes and heaved it up into the prep sink. As I began to rip the bag open to wash the potatoes, my eyes drifted up to look out at the main part of diner. The ghost that had been following me was at the front window, as always, staring me down.

One thing I hadn't told Ginny about working with police—the main reason it's a bad idea—is that you easily become a suspect.

For the purpose of self-preservation, it's always best if the cops think you're a fraud.

CHAPTER 9

The ghost got no more attention from me the rest of the late morning. Setting about cleaning, peeling, and slicing the potatoes into fries, I ignored everything but work. Ginny sliced up onions, pickles, tomatoes, and lettuce to slip into the to-go containers we handed out. Any little bit of vegetable we could get our patrons to eat was a win.

Once I'd gotten all of the potatoes prepared, the two of us worked together forming small hamburger patties. With the price of meat what it is, we quickly realized that everyone would be lucky to get a thin, two-ounce burger. After forming the patties so they'd be ready to fry up, I found a couple of industrial-size cans of baked beans in the pantry. Adding a scoop or two to each to-go box would help increase the protein for our patrons.

Usually, on Saturdays, the folks from the camp were our main customers. A few of the older folks in town would stop by since we were a convenient place to get a quick, cheap meal. Whoever was working at the gas station, and maybe Max, would stop by as well. But it was typically a slow day for us. By the time Sal showed up to get the order for the folks at the camp, we'd already seen all the non-camp folks we'd see all day. Once the camp was taken care of, I was going to tell Ginny we should close up shop.

Fortunately, expecting Sal to come meant we practically had her twenty to-go boxes ready for her in bags when she arrived.

Thinking ahead, she'd brought Ronny-Boy with her to help carry the food back to camp. A bag full of soups and a bag full of grilled cheese sandwiches was one thing. Twenty to-go containers of burgers with fries and beans was another.

As Ronny-Boy took off with two of the bags, Sal was handing me one of the bags from the previous day. A glance inside told me it was the to-go soup containers ready to be washed and reused for the camp. Saving money on containers always made me happy. Technically, laws about safe food handling insisted I toss the used containers. However, I always kept the camp's stuff separate from everything else, they were washed thoroughly, and were only reused for camp patrons. What the Health Board didn't know didn't hurt any of us.

"Thanks, Sal," I said. "We'll get 'em washed up. Chili Monday, so they'll come in use."

Sal smacked her lips. "And cornbread?"

"Of course," I said, handing her the rest of their order. "Probably make up some greens so all of you get your vegetables."

She laughed and took the bags from me before a cloud seemed to cross her face. I found myself standing across the counter from her, staring back at her as she stood there, her arms at her side, a bag dangling from each hand. Ginny was banging around in the back of the diner, obviously getting things cleaned up as quickly as possible so we could cut out early.

"What is it, Sal?" I asked.

"It's Gary," she said with a sigh, slumping.

The bags in her hands nearly touched the floor.

"What about him?" I asked. "He still as sullen as he was earlier today?"

"You noticed?" Sal asked.

"It's hard not to," I said as I gripped the edge of the counter with my hands for a relaxing lean. "Gary's been nothing but grim for…well, a long time. It's been months."

Sal nodded along. "I worry about him."

"Well, sure."

Glancing around furtively, as if someone might sneak up on our conversation, Sal seemed to tense. I glanced around as well, wondering what in the world she was looking for in the diner. With only three people in the diner, I couldn't imagine who Sal thought would overhear anything we were talking about. Or that we were talking about anything worth overhearing.

"Marcella," Sal whisper-hissed suddenly, leaning forward.

I couldn't help but jerk slightly, but I corrected myself quickly.

"The friend that came to camp with Gary when he arrived last year?" I asked.

"Yes," Sal nodded excitedly. "You know, she took off, and he's been getting worse by the day out of worry for her. He was never much of a talker or socializer, but he was functional with her around. But she took off, and, well, now Gary is…*Gary.*"

I studied Sal for a moment as she stood there, the bags drooping at her sides as she looked around nervously.

"He's just…he's acting stranger and stranger by the day," Sal said. "I wish I could help him. You know?"

I was no idiot. Dealing with summoning spirits and the people who wanted to summon them had made me a good nonsense detector.

"You wonder if he has something to do with her disappearance?" I said flatly.

Sal flinched, but didn't deny it.

"Pretty young woman comes to live in the homeless camp with a, well, a guy who doesn't look like someone pretty young women would want to be around...and then she comes up missing after a while. You can't help but wonder if the guy who looks like he shouldn't be around pretty young women had something to do with her disappearance?" I suggested.

"Don't put it that way!" Sal's cheeks reddened.

"Don't try to dance around the obvious," I chuckled. "Just be straight with me, Sal. I talk to ghosts for a living. Once people die, they're not shy about letting you know what they've been thinking their whole lives. I'm pretty unshockable."

She cleared her throat.

"Well," she said, "it does make you wonder, don't it? Marcella suddenly disappearing?"

I shrugged. "I didn't really know her all the well. I only saw her walking around with Gary from time to time. She'd always smile. She tried talking to me a few times, but stopped approaching me after a while. Guess she didn't like me or something?"

"Well," Sal looked nervous, "she probably figured out you were, well, a waste of time?"

I cocked an eyebrow.

"Marcella would depend on strange men to sometimes provide for her and Gary," Sal said, looking anywhere but at me. "She probably figured out quickly that you were a lost cause."

I couldn't help but laugh.

"Well," I said, "she was definitely perceptive. I'm not known for looking to spend time with pretty young women."

Sal gave me an apologetic smile.

"Anyway," Sal continued, hurrying away from the uncomfortable moment, "it's not hard to see how Gary might have gotten jealous or something. Right?"

"Or one of the *strange men* got violent," I said. "Why do you assume Gary had anything to do with her disappearance? It's sad as heck, but young women like Marcella go missing often."

"Well, yes, but—"

"Why do you suspect Gary of doing something to her?" I asked. "He comes in here all the time and never does anything violent to us."

"I don't know, Si," Sal said. "That thing Ginny said the other day, about him coming in here and staring and creeping her out. Sometimes at night, I'll wake up to find him gone, and then see him creep in later and get back to his sleeping spot as if nothing happened. He's been doing sneaky things like that a lot. Disappearing. Reappearing. No longer talking. Lurking around. That kind of thing."

"But has he been violent or weird otherwise?" I asked.

Sal shrugged.

"Sal—"

"Couldn't you just *ask around*?" Sal's eyes roamed around the room. "Talk to some of your ghosts and see if anyone has heard or seen anything?"

"Ghosts don't pay attention to the living much," I said. "Unless it's living people they had business with in life. Or cared about."

Sal nodded.

"You think she's dead," I said.

She nodded once more. Firmly.

I sighed. "Sal...I don't get involved in these things. You know that. If she's dead—and you think Gary had something to do with it—go to the cops. I was literally just telling Ginny hours ago that—"

"They'll come in here and break the whole camp up, arrest everyone they can, run everyone off that isn't arrested—they won't investigate Marcella's disappearance. They won't care about some young homeless woman, and you know it!"

I couldn't help but feel scolded. And rightfully so.

"All's going to the cops will do is ruin everything for everyone down at the camp."

"True."

"If you could just ask around a bit," Sal said. "Just see if any of them ghosts have seen or heard anything. Maybe they saw her leave town on a bus or in someone's car? Maybe there's no crime at all and she just had enough of Sage Grove? Anything. I just need to know we don't have no murderer in the camp or nothing like that."

"What if there is a crime?" I asked. "I won't get involved in that, Sal. Nothing you can say will change that."

What I'd said made me a complete jerk. I was willing to live with it. From experience, I knew getting involved in police business as a medium was asking for nothing but trouble. With the present state of the world, the odds of getting thrown in a jail cell or some detention center, never to be returned to my life, was exponentially higher than ever. If it made me a bad person, so be it, but I wasn't going to ruin my life to solve one murder. Getting thrown in jail wouldn't bring the dead person back, after all.

The "Good Guys" were never the good guys, and they were only getting worse as the years went on. Everyone had to start thinking about self-preservation and the smartest ways to make their way through life. If that made a person a jerk, that was simply too bad. Maybe, one day, when I was a ghost, I'd find out that Heaven actually existed and my choices condemned me to never getting there.

I was willing to risk it.

"If you find out the worst," Sal chewed at her lip, "I'll tell the cops. I won't tell them you had anything to do with figuring it out. I'll just let them know my suspicions and whatever you tell me."

I stared at her.

"I know you get enough guff as it is, Si." Sal moaned. "You feed us, often for free, you tell us the best places to sleep at night without getting caught, and you constantly act like you don't know anything about what we're doing if the cops come sniffing around. I know this is a lot to ask of you, but—"

"I'll ask a few of my dependable ghosts," I said, stopping her. "I won't promise more than that. Fair enough?"

Sal's face immediately lit up.

"Yes!"

I waved a tired arm at her.

"Go on, then," I said. "The food's getting cold and I need to help Ginny close up for the day. We'll talk soon."

Sal practically skipped out of The Lunch Counter, the bags bouncing at her sides. The ghost who had been following me turned to watch her bounce away, confused by the crazy woman. I shook my head and sighed, then turned to head back into the prep area of the diner.

Ginny was standing in the doorway, leaning against the jamb, her arms across her chest.

"You're going to regret all that," she said, shaking her head.

"I already do," I said, laughing. "Let's just get this place cleaned up."

CHAPTER 10

It was like chasing a fly around, trying to get it to go out a window or get close enough to swat. After leaving the diner, I'd stopped at the Gas & Go for another energy drink—I was becoming addicted—and then by the Shop-A-Teria for a box of pasta noodles. Upon arriving home, I put the pasta on the counter to wait for time to cook dinner, and placed the energy drink in the fridge. Then I set about finding and cornering the ghost from the cupboard.

Making one's home ghost proof—*or seemingly ghost proof*—has one glaring disadvantage. When a ghost finds a way around the "proof," you're out of practice when it comes to getting ghosts out of your house. It had been so long since I'd actually found, lured, and captured a ghost that I could barely remember where to start.

Side note – the main key to finding and luring a ghost starts with knowing the ghost's name. You can easily stumble upon a ghost at any old time as a medium. However, if you want to find a *specific ghost*, and command them to speak with you, you have to call them. You can't reliably call a ghost if you don't know their name.

Running around my house like a chicken with my head cut off screaming, "*Hey, you!*" doesn't have the desired effect. The ghost hiding from me could simply think me insane. Which would only make it want to hide better. Ghosts also live in a different style of reality than alive people. Saying something like, *"Ghost hiding in my house! Come here!"* will only confuse a ghost.

How do they know they're the only ghost hiding in the house? And why would they answer to such a rude command anyway? They'd need some sort of motivation to reveal themselves instead of actively hiding. A ghost needs to know you want to help them, deliver a message, take a message from them to deliver, and so forth. It's not necessarily true that all ghosts float around, waiting for someone to notice them and talk to them. Some ghosts, like humans, prefer to be left alone. The ones that hide—the ones that like being left alone—are usually the ones that had a traumatic death.

That's my experience with them, anyway.

After spending an hour after work trying to find the ghost in the house, and only catching the occasional glimpse, I had to give up. Besides, there's a lot more to dealing with a rogue ghost than simply locating it.

INTERLUDE 2

Or...

What they don't teadch you in school about ghosts.

How to Catch a Ghost

Step 1

Acquire a box with one opening and eight pieces of silver.

Step 2

Summon the ghost.
Knowing the ghost's name is critical for ensured success.

Step 3

Tell ghost you wish to help it. Lure it into the box—an item that belonged to the ghost in life helps with this task.

Step 4

Close box quickly. Seal box. Place a piece of silver at all eight corners of the opening to the box.

Step 5

Quickly remove the ghost from the space before it finds its way out of the box. This method is temporary and will surely not hold a ghost forever.

BACK TO OUR REGULARLY SCHEDULED PROGRAM...

I had no idea who the ghost had been in life. So, having an item to lure the ghost out into the open was an insane prospect. How to go about luring the ghost out swirled through my head, but the only resolution I landed on was reaching out to other mediums in our group chat online. Maybe one of them had recently trapped a ghost without knowing its name or having an item that once belonged to it.

As I was considering reaching out to the medium community, another thought occurred to me. I'd already agreed to reach out to somebody else—and I could possibly kill two birds with one stone. However, a long talk had to be had before I could even consider such a thing. Resolved and annoyed, I stomped out of the house and into the backyard. The sun was staring to sink beneath the horizon, so it was a good time to reach out.

"Chester?" I asked in a normal speaking voice.

I didn't like to *summon* Chester unless forced. He always seemed to hang around nearby, so summoning him, or forcing his attention seemed rude. Besides, he was a family member and old friend. Summoning him seemed to go against everything. If forced, I would summon him, but it would be a last resort in a dire situation.

After a few moments, I saw a shimmer at the edge of the woods, which drew my attention. As the sun dipped below the horizon, Chester stepped out of the tree line and floated towards me, his transparent feet barely grazing the ground. His eyes were seeping a bit, but otherwise, he looked good.

"Sorry," I said as he approached, "I should have waited until the sun fully set."

Chester smiled.

"It's fine. It has now set."

103

In the purple rose of dusk, I took a deep breath and decided I had no choice but to do what I'd come out into the yard to do.

"Would you do a favor for me, Chester?" I asked.

His face brightened and the seeping at his eyes stopped.

"A favor? A task? A mission? What is it?"

I couldn't help but grin at his excitement.

"Nothing all that dangerous or thrilling, I'm afraid," I said, holding my hands up.

The seeping at his eyes didn't restart, but I could see a visible change in his level of excitement. However, he seemed to shimmer with curiosity and hope. I don't know what kind of existence ghosts live when I'm not observing them, but a lot of them seem to grow bored after many years of simply floating around. Even getting to do whatever you want whenever you want gets old after a while.

"There's a missing woman in town," I said. "Marcella. I don't know her last name. I don't know if anyone does. But she's one of the homeless people from the camp down by the river? She's come up missing and I promised the leader of the camp I'd see if any of the ghosts around here saw her leave town or…anything."

Chester's eyes lit up once more and the black ooze around his eyes disappeared completely.

"Could you ask around maybe?" I explained. "You don't have to wear yourself out or anything, but if you happen to hear anything or know who to ask, it would be appreciated. If I could give them any information about where she—"

"A mission!" Chester jolted into the air a few feet, then back down, a grin splitting his face. *"Consider it done, Silas!"*

He shimmered and appeared about to zip away, but I stopped him.

"I have one more question," I said.

"Of course, of course, of course!" Chester crowed.

I sighed. "A ghost has found its way into the house."

Chester's eyes grew wide.

"I know!" I threw my hands up.

"How could you let such a thing happen?" Chester gave a ghostly moan.

"It was trapped in a cupboard and a friend let it out," I said, defensively. "It wasn't my fault. I promise."

Chester shook his head and made a "tsk" sound, but kept his thoughts to himself. Only an Erie would shame another Erie from the afterlife.

"Anyway," I said, wondering if I wanted to ask the question now that Chester had shamed me, "I don't know a name or anything. No idea who it is."

Chester grimaced.

"This does not bode well," Chester said. *"You may have to burn the house down!"*

I waved him off quickly.

"No, no, no," I laughed nervously. "It won't come to that. However, I wanted to know…if I let you into the house…"

Chester's eyes grew wide with disbelief.

"Well, would you be able to locate the ghost, find out its name, stuff like that? Things a medium can't do? Well, an *alive* medium can't do?"

Even asking the question I felt like a fool. Suggesting to a ghost, who was a medium in life, that you would willingly let *any* ghost into your house, was insane. Chester's face revealed exactly that thought.

"You should never *let a ghost into the house, Silas Erie! Ever!"*

"I understand that, Chester," I said. "But you'd leave willingly for me after you found out the ghost's name, right?"

Chester's displeased, judgmental expression disappeared suddenly and he seemed to think on that question for a moment.

"*Well,*" he said slowly, "*I suppose that I would. Other ghosts would not, but I would, yes.*"

"So," I asked again, "if it comes to it, would you let me trap you, bring you inside, release you, let you find and talk to the ghost, then let me trap you and release you outside again?"

Chester flinched every time I said "trap," but managed to keep his composure.

"*I suppose…yes. If it becomes a necessity.*"

"Only if it's necessary," I said, nodding with a smile. "I'll do my best to figure it out on my own so that it doesn't become necessary, though. I just wanted to know if you'd be willing and if it would be possible."

"*Willing and possible.*" Chester nodded.

"Thanks, Chester," I said.

Dusk had begun to settle into night around us. The chill of an autumn night was prickling at my bare arms and neck.

"Okay," I said. "I'll leave you to check about Marcella and whatever else you have going on. Thanks, Chester."

With an excited expression at the reminder he had a mission, Chester gave me a grand nod of his head—which nearly rolled off his shoulders—then he was zipping away back towards the woods. His body shimmered more brightly than I'd seen it do in weeks, which made me smile.

Wrapping my arms around myself and running my hands up and down the bare flesh, I could feel that autumn was settling in for good. It wouldn't be long before the leaves all turned brown, yellow, and orange before falling to create a carpet in the woods behind the house. Then, when winter set in, everything around my house would become a winter wonderland with ghosts zipping in and around the trees like fireflies.

I'm not certain what it is about winter that makes ghosts appear more frequently, but it does. Possibly, the temporary death of the world as it falls into its wintry slumbers calls out to the dead? It's their season to frolic and make merriment before the long sunny days return and life returns to the world around them. Ghosts are drawn to the living, but not life.

Figure that one out.

When I turned back to the house, I nearly toppled over backward. Danny was standing in the shadows of the back porch. The blue light on his vape pen lit up before he chuckled with laughter and blew out a plume of blueish vapor.

"Too bad you can't sense humans," Danny said. "You wouldn't have been so startled."

"Well, I should have sensed you," I said, gripping my chest with my hand. "You move like the dead."

"Silent like ninja!" Danny proclaimed.

"I'm not sure if that's offensive," I said, stepping over to him, "but that vape definitely is."

I attempted to pry the vape pen from his hand, but he quickly deposited it into his hip pocket. As if that would keep me from getting to it. Obviously, Danny also was aware of this fact.

"If you want it, you'll have to go in after it," he grinned evilly in the darkness of the porch.

I rolled my eyes.

"Are you here for dinner, or just the floor show? Because I need to eat first." I asked.

Danny frowned at me.

"Have I mischaracterized our situation?" I teased. "Or was my honesty tacky?"

"That's not what this is," Danny said.

"Sure," I said with a nod. "I'm making pasta. Nothing fancy. But there will be salad and garlic bread, so well-rounded meal and all that, I suppose."

I stepped around him to open the backdoor. Danny grabbed my forearm and stopped me.

"That's not what this is," he said again.

"And I can't see ghosts," I said.

We stared at each other for longer than was comfortable.

"You can convince yourself of anything if you really want to believe it," I said with finality.

Danny said nothing.

"So?" I asked brightly. "Pasta? Salad? Garlic bread?"

He gave a firm nod.

"Great," I said. "Follow me."

And I led us into the house.

CHAPTER 11

Danny's fingers were playing along my bare shoulder when I woke the next morning, the sunlight assaulting the drapes. I laid there for several minutes, my eyes barely open against the onslaught of day as Danny ran his fingers along my flesh. Between the central heat and the warm blankets, I felt flushed and his fingers felt like fire on my skin. A delicious fire that threatened to spread if I didn't stop him before it caught.

"You know, we could just stay in bed all day," Danny murmured, propped up on one elbow beside me in bed.

He was on the side closest to the window, blocking any draft that might somehow sneak into the house. That only made me feel cozier and warmer.

"The Lunch Counter can stay closed for one day," he cooed. "And you would only have to cook for two today."

I looked up at him, amused.

"I never cook breakfast at the diner," I said. "And The Lunch Counter is always closed on Sundays."

He frowned down at me; his head cocked to the side.

"If you paid attention to me when I wasn't nude, you'd know that," I said.

"Don't start that," he grinned and leaned down to kiss my forehead. "I thought we finished that over dinner."

Ignoring a conversation while we filled ourselves with carbs and minimal vegetables was not finishing a topic in my mind.

However, it was early, I was starting to wake up, and I didn't want to begin the day annoyed.

"Well, it's closed," I said. "I wasn't leaving the house today, anyway."

"What I'm hearing is you're free to whip up a breakfast to help me recharge," Danny said.

He laid back his hands behind his head, a sly grin on his face.

"You know," I replied as I rolled over under the covers to look at him, "someone has to help the people in this town who can't help themselves."

He rolled his eyes, though I could tell he wasn't being completely dismissive. I'd known Danny long enough to know that he didn't hold a single bad thought in his head for the unhoused and struggling populations of Sage Grove. The town itself is what held his ire. The citizens were simply collateral damage to that anger.

"Who will help people if The Lunch Counter wasn't there?" I asked.

"Who's going to help them when the last business in this town finally shutters and the town becomes deserted by everyone but them?" he asked.

I stared at him.

"Are you going to stay here and wither away with them?" he asked, looking over at me. "Or are you finally going to look out for number one?"

"Well," I said softly, "it would be a lot easier to look after the people in this town if certain people stopped shuttering the buildings, right?"

"Not this again." Danny groaned. "Mom hasn't closed up any more of the buildings she owns since Dad died. That was all him. She isn't doing anything to hurt the people down at the camp and you know it."

"She's not helping as much as she could," I mumbled and laid back.

"Dad closed that run down inn," Danny said. "So what? Mom owns fifteen other buildings in this crap town and she isn't doing anything with them, including closing them off. They're just tax write-offs to her at this point. She doesn't care who's sleeping in them at night."

"The county is posting—"

"She can't stop the county from posting notices," Danny grumbled, sitting up in bed. "You know, she pays you five days a week to swindle her so you can make food for them, free of charge. I'm not expecting you to give her a crown and throw a parade, but she's doing more than anyone else in this hellhole. Except, maybe, you. Let it go."

I took a deep breath, steadying myself, swallowing my anger, before sitting up.

"I'm not swindling her," I said simply. "Your dad never appears when I try to summon him for her."

Danny wasn't unamused, but he rolled his eyes.

"Swindler," he said.

He was teasing, but it cut deep.

"Believe what you want," I said.

"Make me a believer then, Si," he said. "Prove to me you can talk to ghosts."

I stared at him, then down at my lap.

"Summon my dad," he said. "Right now."

"Ghosts can't come in the house," I replied, simply.

"That's not true," Danny chided me. "There's one in here now, according to you. Came in via the cupboard. Right?"

"Right," I gave him a nod.

He snorted. "So?"

"It found a loophole."

"Then let's go outside," Danny said. "Okay. Ghosts can't get into the house without a *loophole*. Let's go outside. Right now. Summon my dad. Talk to him. Make me a believer."

Reaching down, I grabbed my boxers and slid them on, then stood from the bed. When I got to the bedroom door, I turned and looked over my shoulder at my still naked…whatever…in my bed, watching me expectantly. The mix of desperation, sadness, and a sprinkle of disbelief in his eyes pained me.

"You coming?" I asked.

"We're…you're going to summon Dad?"

"I'm going to make you breakfast."

Then I turned and left my bedroom. I'd gotten out some sausages, put bread in the toaster, and retrieved the eggs and butter from the fridge before Danny entered the kitchen. Seeing that he'd only put on his boxers and socks let me know that I hadn't upset him enough to make him want to leave, even after breakfast. I was pleased, but also unsure if I wanted to be pleased.

Having Danny stick around the house all day and enjoy the things I *would* do for him excited me. Knowing that, eventually, we'd both realize that it would never be enough, made me sad. One day, maybe so far in the future that it ruined the life we both could have had, things would end. There would be no changing it or fixing it.

My brain told me that I was intentionally setting myself up for heartache. Something else, that I wasn't so proud to be taking advice from, told me to see how it all played out.

Danny sat at the table, his legs spread out in that way that only guys who haven't been beaten down by life enough spread their legs, and waited. I toasted and buttered the bread liberally, fried up the sausages, and scrambled eggs with some Fontina cheese and chives and butter. Finally, I set two plates on the kitchen table. One in front of Danny, and one in the seat across from him.

He smacked his lips, looking down at his plate. Before he could grab his fork, I took his face in my hands and let them slide up to his hair. I stroked his soft brown hair and pushed his head back to look up at me.

"Did you like your father when he was alive?" I asked.

Danny stared up at me. He said nothing.

"What makes you think you'd like anything he had to say now?"

Danny's eyes darted away for a moment, then settled back on mine.

"Death doesn't change people," I said, softly. "There's no great reveal at the end of life that makes a person rethink their ways. To revisit their transgressions or hurts. They aren't punished for any pain they caused others—not that I've seen. They're not suddenly honest or forthright. They don't suddenly become upstanding human-like beings just because they died. They don't always plead for forgiveness and understanding and seek out those they wronged and make things right."

Danny's eyes bore into mine.

"In fact," I said, gently stroking his head to ease what I was about to say, "death, from what I've seen, reminds them that there are no real consequences left. Death can make people even worse."

He looked down but my fingers stayed twirling in his hair, attempting to comfort him.

"It's the uncommon soul who sees death as a second chance."

I let my hand slide from his hair, caressed the side of his face gently, then slid into the chair across from him. Picking up my fork, I wasn't sure I was even hungry, but I dug into my eggs. I didn't even manage to lift the fork from my plate before Danny spoke.

"Are you scared of the idea of dying since you're a medium?" he asked quietly.

When I looked up, he was staring at me apprehensively.

"No," I snorted. "It makes me more afraid of living."

My statement seemed to affect Danny in a physical way and an expression I'd never seen on his face before flashed for a split second. He looked down at his plate, grabbed his fork and jabbed at a sausage.

"You could always move up to Dubuque," he said. "It's less than an hour. I mean…be closer to me. I wouldn't have to keep coming down here so often. The internet is everywhere. You could do business there, too. Your sister ran away from this town. You could, too."

"And leave all this?" I waved my hands grandly. "I'm rent-free, baby."

Danny chuckled, and I joined in. Then we both dug into our plates.

CHAPTER 12

Danny left in the early afternoon. But only after we'd spent a few more hours in bed and he got a free lunch off of me. He took a shower after the meal and headed out, promising to see me soon. As always with Danny, I prepared myself for that goodbye to be the last, and saw him off with as much pleasantness as I could muster.

Knowing that I had an afternoon and the evening to myself, I focused on my mission. Finding the ghost in the house and trying to, at the minimum, figure out its name and where it had come from, was paramount. If possible, knowing that much would help me develop a method for trapping it so that I could get it out of the house. With that information, I felt it was possible I could even get it to allow itself to be trapped and transferred outside where it would have more freedom to roam.

You can convince yourself of anything if you really want to believe it.

Even if you're a medium.

However, after several hours of scouring the house, every nook and cranny, and even attempting to summon the ghost in a plethora of ways, I was unsuccessful. Dust bunnies that I'd been meaning to clear out for far too long were addressed in the process, so it wasn't a total loss. However, the sun was setting when I finally admitted to myself that I had failed once again.

I found myself making another simple dinner—a quick salad topped with grilled chicken, before heading out to the atrium. Candlelight was illuminating the room and the blue glow of my laptop was casting my face in a sickly hue when I took the first bite of my dinner. The ghost that had been following me forever was standing in the corner, behind a spider plant, glowering at me as I ate and ignored it.

"Talk toooooo meeeee."

I ignored it, taking another bite of my salad. My hard and fast rule is I summon ghosts is that they do not summon me.

Going through my email, I found that I'd gotten quite a few requests for summonings throughout the day. Fortunately, more than half were not prepaid, so I was able to shoot off several emails that I'd be happy to help the client with their spirit-summoning needs once a payment had been made. Those requests were moved aside, leaving me a measly five requests to complete before I could have my night to myself.

My first summoned ghost answered questions about a missing family locket—an heirloom apparently—and asked that a message be forwarded to her daughter. An easy enough job for the money paid. The second and third summonings were fairly common as well. Questions about family happenings and messages to be relayed, so I wasn't too bothered by them, either.

The fourth summoning was one of the more problematic requests that, unfortunately, I receive far too often. From reading the email, I already knew that the person requesting the summoning was simply testing my abilities. They wanted me to contact someone they knew had passed on, get information that only the ghost would know to prove I was the real deal, and then relay it back to them.

These types of jobs severely annoy me. So, I did what I always did when I had such a client. I summoned the ghost, received the information I needed, and forwarded it back to the client. Then I opened a spreadsheet on my laptop and added the email to a list of "special" clients. If they ever emailed back from the same address and asked for further work, they would be charged a much higher rate than any other client who was simply looking for closure or answers. Everyone in the spreadsheet paid at least fifty-percent more than any other client.

I felt perfectly fine with this practice. Waste my time, I waste your money. Simple as that.

The final ghost summoned for the evening turned out to be a Screamer. One of the ghosts that was so freshly dead and traumatized by the experience that it couldn't remember anything and all it does is scream, wail, and moan. They're the absolute worst. Not simply because they are annoying, but because I always refund the client's money and have to explain why I couldn't help them at this time.

In those emails, I explain to clients that if they want to try back in a few months, the ghost may be more talkative. I will happily try again at the same rate that they paid at the time of the first summoning, but at the current time, I was unable to help them with their request. Many clients understood, but some of them simply labeled me a fraud and never tried to contact their deceased loved one. At least, through me.

One of the drawbacks of dealing with the dead for a living.

After composing the email and issuing a refund, I had to spend another half hour convincing the Screamer to leave the atrium. When a ghost is carrying on to such a degree, it's difficult to get them to even hear you, let alone listen. Fortunately, the Screamer wasn't one of the worst I'd ever dealt with. A half hour to solve a Screamer problem in the atrium isn't the most time I've spent solving a problem like that, so I felt lucky.

As I was wrapping things up for the evening, I checked the clock on my laptop. There was still an hour and a half before bedtime. Having some time to watch a bit of television with a snack always made my evening better after summonings. It helps to bring myself out of the world of the dead and back into the world of the living.

When I closed my laptop, blew out the candle, and headed back to the house, I was interrupted by a sudden cold ghost of wind. Turning to see what had caused the gust, since the atrium door to outside was closed and locked, I jumped back with surprise. Chester was floating before me in the atrium, half of his spirit form in the middle of the table. He looked as though he had popped out of the table like a jack in the box.

Chuckling to myself as I took him in, I removed my hand from the knob to the house door and approached him. Chester looked grave, though I suppose all ghosts do when you think about it. Black ooze was dribbling from the corners of his mouth and his eyes looked more sunken than usual. Typically, such a look on Chester meant he had been concerned or busy with something that bothered him. That thought made my brow furrow as I stood before him.

"What's up, Chester?" I asked.

"*A ghost saw a dead woman's body.*" Chester said, not bothering to find a gentler way into the conversation. "*You told me to look for a dead woman.*"

My heart sank.

"Marcella?" I asked quickly.

"*I do not know,*" Chester said. "*Oliphius told me that he saw the body.*"

Oliphius, like Chester, was a ghost. Obviously. However, he was a Haunt, spending all of his time in downtown Sage Grove. If there was a body or another ghost in his territory, it would only make sense that he would be the one to report it to Chester if Chester went around talking to all of the ghosts. I wasn't as familiar with Oliphius as Chester was. However, every time I'd encountered him, he seemed as reliable as any other ghost.

Which is to say—reliable, but use caution when believing everything they say.

Even Chester's memory could not be fully trusted.

"Let me get my keys," I said quickly. "You can take me to Oliphius and—"

"*He can't remember where it was,*" Chester said, cutting me off with his ethereal voice.

He was bobbing up and down, sinking further into and then rising out of the table in front of me, as though on a short spring.

"What do you mean?" I asked.

Chester bobbled a moment before stopping.

"*Oliphius has no memory,*" Chester explained. "*He can remember events, but places and time...*"

The ooze at the corners of his mouth dribbled off, dropping to the ground, and disappeared before hitting the table.

"When did he see the body?" I asked the obvious question.

No one had reported a woman missing in Sage Grove in quite a while. The only person that I knew that was missing was Marcella, but that hadn't exactly been "reported." When an unhoused person—in general—is missing, it doesn't get reported. Other unhoused people are reluctant to go to the cops and the general public doesn't care enough to say anything.

119

It's a sad, yet true, fact about unhoused people and how they are treated by society.

"*Maybe,*" Chester thought about the question, "*a week ago. Or a month. Last Christmas?*"

I wanted to roll my eyes at Chester, but knew better. He was trying his best, and only relaying what Oliphius had told him. Ghosts have no real sense of time. You don't watch the calendar or count the days when time no longer means anything, after all.

"Oh."

Chester's head bobbled.

"Well, does he have any thoughts on where it might have been?" I asked the logical question.

"*He does not,*" Chester answered immediately.

"Crap." I exhaled the word.

Chester nodded to the affirmative once more.

"*I will ask more of my friends,*" Chester declared. "*I will not rest until I have found this woman for you.*"

I did my best to give him a warm smile as he began bobbing up and down like a fishing bobber again.

"Rest tonight, Chester," I said. "You've worked hard and found something to start. You've done well. Don't overwork yourself."

Chester considered what I said.

"*I will begin my search tomorrow.*"

"Sounds great," I said. "Thank you. Go rest."

He gave a bow, turned, and immediately breezed through the table and the atrium wall, back out to the woods. Even ghosts need to give their brains a rest. No. I don't know how that works or why ghosts aren't full of infinite energy. But everything needs to recharge from time to time.

I sighed, and watched Chester disappear into the woods. Then, with nothing else to do, I turned and went into the house.

CHAPTER 13

"I'm tired of this place," Ginny grumbled as she stirred the giant pot of chili.

Sweat was beading on her forehead as I mixed a giant bowl of cornbread batter on the table next to her. Her arm was working overtime to get to the bottom of the pot and stir the chili thoroughly. The heat coming off of the oven would have been welcome if you'd just come into the diner. It was turning out to be a chilly day—perfect for what we had on the menu at The Lunch Counter. However, being trapped in the diner with the heat and steam for longer than a few minutes was oppressive. I hadn't started sweating yet, but I knew it was the inevitable conclusion.

"Can't we do something about the heat in here?" Ginny finished stirring the pot and waved a hand in front of her like a hummingbird's wings.

"That's these old buildings in town for you," I sighed, continuing to mix the batter. "They were made to keep heat in. We can turn the central lower if you want?"

Not waiting for clearer permission, Ginny dashed over to the thermostat and turned the heat down to sixty degrees. Of course, I knew that it would do no good. That's not how central heat works—it only comes on if the temperate in a building falls lower than what is specified. Unless we opened the front door, there was no chance of cooling things off. Not until we stopped cooking and the stove was shut off.

"Go open the door and let a bit of cold air in," I suggested.

Ginny agreed with a firm nod and rounded the counter to do as instructed. As soon as she opened the front door, an arctic blast of cold air blew through the front room of the diner. Immediate relief flooded me as the cold air caused a shiver to run up my back. Ginny stuck her head outside and breathed deeply, a satisfied groan emanating from her throat.

After a minute of this pose, she fanned the door a few times. Gusts of air gushed into the diner, and finally, Ginny let go of the door, letting it glide shut gently. We both smiled at each other now that the diner felt like it was a reasonable temperature.

As Ginny returned to the counter and sat down on one of the stools, I began to pour the cornbread batter into greased muffin tins. Once all of the tins were prepared, I quickly opened the oven and shoved them all in, one by one, as rapidly as I could without tipping them out. Then I slammed the oven shut and groaned.

"How is it so cold outside and so hot in here?" Ginny lamented. "I mean, I know, I know, the building traps in heat, but you'd think some would get out. Or some cold would get in. But, Si, this is ridiculous."

"Well," I said, "if I had money, I'd pay a contractor to come check things out and see if there's a ventilation problem or something we could do, but we're not rolling in the dough here."

My partner gave me a sympathetic look.

"I know there's nothing you can do about it, buddy," she said, reassuring me. "I'll be happy when winter comes, anyway."

"For sure," I said. "They're predicting a bad one this year."

She rolled her eyes and laid her head on her hands on the counter.

"Can't win, can you?" I chuckled.

Mumbling some response into her hands that I couldn't quite catch, I simply laughed at her. I gave my hands a quick, yet thorough, wash in the sink next to the table and dried them on the kitchen towel stuck into the tie of my apron. I removed the apron and towel and laid them on the counter next to Ginny's head, causing her to look up.

"Is it that late already?" She sat up to look at the clock on the wall.

"Time to swindle my best customer," I said.

"Are you admitting something, or taking a jab at me?" Ginny put her hands on her hips and waggled her head.

We both laughed.

"I get money, she doesn't get to talk to her husband," I said with a shrug. "It's a swindle even if it's not my fault."

Ginny grinned. "Fair enough."

"I'll be back in an hour," I replied. "Unless we get the shock of our lives and Harlan decides to make an appearance for once."

"You'll be back in an hour," Ginny said in a sing-song voice as I rounded the corner and walked past her.

She spun on the stool to watch me as I retrieved my coat and scarf from the coat tree by the front door. Though she said nothing as I put the scarf around my neck and shrugged on my coat, I knew something was on her mind. My best friend and partner in culinary crimes was never silent. Typically, whatever was on her mind fell out of her mouth like a watermelon from a skyscraper.

"What is it?" I asked. "I can tell you want to say something."

Chewing at her lip, Ginny said, "I know I've only worked here for a year, and I haven't known you much longer than that."

"Yeah?" I rested my hand on the doorhandle.

"Everyone said you could talk to the dead," Ginny continued, "before I even started here. I mean, everyone knows. At least, they talk about it."

"People do love to talk," I said. "But since I run an online business, it's not like it's a secret."

Ginny closed her eyes for a moment, as if steeling up courage.

"You really can talk to ghosts, right?" she blurted out. "You're not a swindler?"

"Want me to summon one of your dead relatives?" I asked, blandly.

Ginny blinked at me.

"Would that make you feel better about me as a person?"

"I don't think—"

"Everyone thinks it," I said with a shrug. "I'm not hurt that you might think it, too."

"I don't think you're a bad person," Ginny said. "But even the best people aren't perfect."

"You don't have to tell me that." I chuckled.

Ginny cocked an eyebrow at me. With a sigh, I squeezed the doorhandle and considered my options.

"If you ever feel that you can't trust me, and you really need proof," I said slowly, "I will summon someone for you."

"I—"

"Free of charge," I said. "If that's what you really need to trust me."

Ginny's cheeks grew red.

"If that's what you need to keep working here," I added.

125

"That's not what I meant," Ginny replied quickly. "I wasn't trying to say—"

I waved her off.

"You're not the first friend to doubt me," I said. "I'm used to it. I'll be back in an hour."

With that, I pulled the door open and slipped out. With the door struggling to slide shut behind from the force of the wind, I pulled my coat more tightly around myself. Plowing into the force of the wind, I took off on my near daily walk to Rhonda's house.

As I made my way down the block, though the walk was short, I realized I had an unfortunate amount of time to consider what had happened. Over the course of my life—at least the part where I'd learned I could see and talk to ghosts—I'd had plenty of similar interactions. Not only with strangers, but with the people closest to me. Many of those people were no longer close to me.

When someone who knows you finds out that you claim you can talk to ghosts, particular things happen. At first, everyone falls into one of two categories. They are excited, or they wonder what medication you should be on. Most people fall in the medication column.

Which isn't an unreasonable place to go with your thoughts when someone mentions talking to ghosts. Certain antipsychotics, anxiolytics, and even some antidepressants can suppress whatever part of the brain it is that allows a medium to see and hear dead people. It doesn't mean that we are schizophrenic, anxious, or depressed—though a lot of mediums have mental health problems, for obvious reasons—but they can partially work to turn off the ghosts.

Because the parts of the brain they affect that cause mental health issues also control one's ability to be a medium. There have been near to nil studies about this. The reason for this is that modern science has no interest in believing that mediums are real. Believing us would be the very first step in getting actual, real scientific studies done on our brains.

Not that I'd volunteer for one.

In the other column—the excited people—are the ones who love ghost stories and horror and are often highly religious, spiritual, or into nature worship. Like Wiccans. Or vegans and people who love to take ten-mile nature hikes on the weekend instead of binging a streaming show.

You know, weirdos.

There can also be a third column—the outliers. Those who are skeptical, but are educated and intelligent enough to understand that without proof, they can neither believe or disbelieve something they haven't experienced. They often treat mediums with polite distance or simply don't mention the medium's abilities when dealing with them on a personal level.

That's fine by me. If you are skeptical and don't want to talk about it, I'll ignore your dead relative screaming in my ear to pass along a message to you. I never force belief or messages on anyone who doesn't want them. Or isn't ready to receive them. Because many people want messages, but if I know for certain it's not the right time to be delivered, I will use my own judgment.

I don't feel bad for reserving the right to pass along messages or summon someone. It's not the ghost or the person they have a connection with that will suffer if things go south. The medium is the one who will be vilified, ridiculed, or even face violence. Beyond that, some messages, from my experience, can cause more problems than they solve.

Sometimes it's better not knowing some things.

Regardless of which column a person falls into, over time, the skepticism creeps into everyone's cracks. Even your most ardent supporters begin to side eye and whisper about you. Unless they see constant proof that you commune with the dead, or feel that every message you pass along is perfect, they will begin to doubt you.

If you refuse to treat your abilities like a party trick, the doubt begins. If you won't summon certain people who have nothing to do with the client, they will doubt you. And, worst of all, if you have no interest in working with the police, the doubt begins.

I will not come to your dinner party, thinking I'm being treated to a meal, only to find out my entrance fee is a séance. I will not summon Marilyn Monroe so you can ask her about JFK. And I will not put myself and others in potential danger to help the police. Could you imagine everyone knowing you have a one-hundred percent success rate finding bodies and who killed the person?

I'd constantly have a price on my head. I'd never be safe anywhere.

No, thank you, please.

If you want to have a decent life as a medium, you have to do one of two things. Ignore your abilities, or become comfortable dealing with the doubt and skepticism of even those closest to you. You have to understand that even the people who love and care about you most may feel you're full of horse crap.

It's part of the gig.

As I approached Rhonda's mansion, Danny's truck came into view. Immediately, I was tempted to turn around and head back to the diner. However, the wind had already turned my cheeks red and my fingers into icicles. The thought of

Rhonda's oppressively warm front room, with all of the candles aglow, was more tempting.

I let myself in through the gate, dashed up the walk, and made my way up the stairs to the front door. Since she had company, it took Rhonda a little bit longer to come to the door. However, it wasn't too long before the door flew open and Rhonda was screaming and ushering me inside. I followed her, as I always did, while she proclaimed to know that this particular day was the day we'd be successful.

I knew better. Even mediums can grow to be skeptics.

As she dragged me into the front room, I was focused on her and removing my coat and scarf. So, we'd been standing in the doorway of the room, as I listened to her talk, for several moments before I looked over at the sofa she typically sat on. I kept my face neutral somehow as I took in Danny sitting there, crossed-legged and tense, watching us.

"I just know that one day you're going to—" Rhonda cut off.

She looked at my eyes and then followed their gaze over to her son. Lighting up with excitement, she clapped her hands with glee.

"Oh," she said, "I hope you don't mind, Silas. I invited my son to sit in on this session."

"I see," I said.

Danny gave me a polite nod.

"You remember him, don't you?" she asked, pulling me towards the sofa and practically shoving me into it.

I laid my coat and scarf over the back of the couch and settled in, trying to look comfortable. Keeping my eyes on Rhonda standing next to me, I ignored Danny.

"You two were in high school together," Rhonda said. "It hasn't been that long. Surely you—"

"Of course," I said, managing a small smile and nod at Danny. "How have you been?"

"Danny," Rhonda said, reminding me.

"How have you been, Danny?" I asked.

Danny managed a small smile.

"I've been great," he said. "You?"

I gestured vaguely. "Can't complain."

Rhonda chortled and glided over to sit down on the sofa next to Danny. She reached over and patted his knee, but Danny's eyes stayed on mine for a moment before he glanced over at his mother and smiled at her. A better smile than he'd given me.

"I don't know," Rhonda said, looking at her son, "but I thought maybe if Danny was also here…"

I watched her hand on his knee for a moment and how they were staring at each other. There was so much hope there. It both broke my heart and angered me. I wasn't so certain that it was Rhonda's idea to invite her son. Danny planting the seed in her mind was definitely likely.

His mother didn't even know that we'd been seeing each other since high school. I was his little secret. I didn't even know if Rhonda knew that her son preferred the company of other men. However, I'd respected that Danny liked to keep his private life private. So, inserting himself in my private moments with his mother made my blood pressure rise.

It wasn't the central heat and dozens of burning candles in the front room that was warming me up quickly.

"Of course," I said as naturally as possible. "Maybe it will make Harlan more likely to want to appear."

You're wasting your time, I thought to myself. *Harlan isn't going to appear. Just as he hasn't since he croaked.*

"And him being here gave us time to have a good catch-up talk," Rhonda said, patting Danny's knee in an admonishing way now. "Every time he comes down, he pops in for a quick chat, then he's off to God only knows where again."

I chuckled. Because it was expected of me. Mother makes a joke about her son not spending enough time with her. Comedy. All that.

"I was talking to Mom about the Inn," Danny said, turning his head to look at me.

Somehow, I managed to keep my face neutral, yet inquisitive, as though I had no idea about the inn.

"Oh?" I asked.

"Danny," Rhonda sighed, rolling her eyes with a chuckle, "seems to think it might be better to open it back up. Not take the doors off or anything, but maybe it would be a place for the local homeless people to use as shelter when it gets too cold this winter."

"That's nice," I said, cocking a discreet eyebrow at Danny.

He gave me a surreptitious shrug while Rhonda was distracted.

"But," Rhonda said, "Harlan closed that up before he died. I just can't bring myself to do it. He didn't want anyone messing with its beauty and history. I can't open it back up."

I choked back my first thought and responded the way I was supposed to respond.

"That's understandable," I said.

I shot a look at Danny, but he was keeping his face neutral as well.

"All of those lovely, historic rooms," Rhonda said wistfully, then suddenly had a thought and sat forward. "Have you ever stayed at the inn? I know it has been closed for a while, but…"

"No," I said. "Never had a reason to. But when I was a kid and things were still kind of booming around here, I remember a lot of people in and out of there. Raving about it."

She was nodding along excitedly.

"So gorgeous," she proclaimed. "Every room a different gorgeous, rich color theme. The burgundy room. Gold room. Teal room. On and on. Beautiful old furniture. All of the rooms had en suites. I'm sad to know that it is going unused, but the utilities are off now, anyway. And there is no reason to turn them back on. Who would come stay?"

The homeless could stay, I thought.

"That would pay for the privilege, anyway." Rhonda chuckled, as though reading my thoughts.

A strained chuckle escaped my mouth and I felt like a jerk. Danny joined in, but I could tell his heart wasn't in it. Rhonda looked around wistfully, then focused her attention back on me. She slid back in her seat and got comfortable, then her hand returned to her son's knee. My eyes darted to the corner of the room when the ghost caught my attention.

"Shall we try summoning Harlan again?" she asked. "Get started?"

"Sure," I said, staring at the ghost in the corner, ignoring her. "Your mother has already joined us again. Are you sure you don't want to talk to her?"

Danny frowned deeply at me, then turned his head to see where my eyes were pointed. He stared at the corner for a moment, then whipped his head back around to look at me.

"No," Rhonda said firmly. "In fact, ask her to leave my house."

A barrage of curses and insults came from the ghost in the corner—none that I hadn't heard from the ghost before.

"She knows you don't want her here," I said, turning my attention back to Rhonda. "She hears you."

"But she won't listen," Rhonda said, shaking her head with a rueful smile.

"No."

"Nana is here?" Danny interjected. "Why don't you ask her something?"

His eyes were pleading with his mom. I knew it wasn't because he loved his grandmother. He wanted to test me now that he had the chance. I was going to leave the decision up to Rhonda—she was the paying customer. Though I was seething from the thought that Danny had joined our session simply to get confirmation of my abilities.

"I do not want that woman in my house," Rhonda said through clenched teeth.

"Can I ask her something?" Danny asked desperately. "Please?"

Rhonda rolled her eyes and gestured vaguely at him. Danny turned to me quickly.

"What is she wearing?" he whipped his head around to me. "What is my Nana wearing?"

"That's…not a question," I said.

"Just tell me," Danny barked.

I stared at him for a moment, trying to decide if I'd refuse to answer his question, simply out of spite. However, I wasn't sure how this would go over with my most reliable, well-paying customer. So, after staring daggers into Danny for a moment, I turned to look at the old woman, who was still cursing at the back of Rhonda's head.

I took stock of Danny's grandmother's appearance, then turned back to stare at him.

"Dark suit," I said. "Navy, I believe. Straight leg pants with a crisp pleat in front. I believe a white silk blouse with a cowl neck under the suit jacket, also navy. White buttons at the cuffs. An impressive pearl necklace with a cameo. Navy ballet flats. Her hair is pulled back, I think in a chignon. She's looking at me, but it's a bun or chignon, I think from how her hair is pulled back. She wanted to be buried in the caftan dress with the butterflies that she always wore after church when she'd sit out on the back porch with her half-lemonade-half-tea and smoke Pall Malls."

I answered Danny's question and delivered grandma's grievance with Rhonda all in one go. Danny stared at me and Rhonda laughed a windchime like laugh.

"Can you imagine, Danny!" Rhonda chuckled. "Burying Mother in that monstrosity? What would people have said?"

Danny said nothing as peals of laughter poured from his mother. Instead, he stared at me, blank faced.

"She wants you to donate her box of caftans to a nursing home," I added. "Because a caftan is an older woman's best comfort in a world that slowly becomes more uncomfortable. Except the butterfly one. She wants that left at her gravesite."

Rhonda laughed harder.

"I got rid of those years ago!" she chuckled, mocking the ghost.

With a poof, Nana Milner disappeared in a cloud of anger. She was there, then she was gone. And Danny was staring at me, ghostly pale. I let Rhonda's laughter die off as I stared at Danny. Finally, when his color began to return, and Rhonda was settling down again, I gave them a tight smile.

"Do you want to try Harlan again?" I asked. "I'd hate to let the whole hour go by and forget to try."

"Yes," Rhonda said, still smiling. "Let's try."

CHAPTER 14

As a medium, one often finds that they are their own worst enemy. Thanks to my interaction with Nana Milner, Rhonda begged me to stay twice as long for three times the pay. As long as I kept trying to summon Harlan, she wanted to keep trying. After two hours of having her wring her hands and hope for the best, and Danny staring at me as though I was a monster, I told Rhonda it was time to give up.

Danny seemed ghostly himself as the session ended, but Rhonda was her usual chipper self. She saw me out of the house after I gave Danny a quick, polite "goodbye." As I left, she stuffed money in my hand and thank me, shutting the door unceremoniously in my face.

When I returned to the diner, later than usual after a session at Rhonda's, Ginny was serving a lunch to David Honeycutt, the manager and owner of the Wash-A-Teria laundromat, our postman, and honorary mayor in Sage Grove. I went and took my coat and scarf off, hanging them on the tree by the door, said "hello" to David, then went and washed my hands. By the time I'd dried my hands and returned to the counter with Ginny, David was gone.

"I guess Harlan finally showed himself?" Ginny asked, looking at the clock.

"Sorry, I'm late," I said. "No. He didn't show up. Again. But her son Danny was there. Gave him a message from his grandmother. So…there's that."

Ginny grinned.

"That's good, right? Proving you aren't a fraud?"

I smiled tightly.

"So," I said, "what needs doing?"

"Actually," Ginny said, "A lot have come and gone already. Chili and cornbread served up and gone."

She gestured at the pots on the stove. One was empty and the burner turned off and the other was half-empty, simmering away still.

"What about Sal?"

"She came by," Ginny replied. "I took care of the order. She asked if you'd had a chance to *ask around* about Marcella."

"Okay," I said. "I guess I'll talk to her about it tomorrow."

"Have you?" Ginny asked, excitedly. "Talked to ghosts about her being missing?"

"Maybe," I replied. "I don't know anything. Honestly, it's not high on my list of priorities. Unhoused people relocate, take off, whatever, all the time. Gary being upset doesn't necessarily mean something is wrong. It just means he misses her."

Ginny cringed.

"Am I getting in your business too much? I'm sorry, Si."

I waved her off.

"It's just…that's business. A different business. It's what I do to make a living. I don't like…I don't want to mix the dead with my life more than I have to."

"I guess I understand," she said. "I'm sorry."

"Stop apologizing," I said with a genuine laugh. "Let's just forget it."

"Well," Ginny said, "if you want, I can clean up and close up for the day."

"Really?" I asked. "You've been doing that a lot lately. I feel like I'm taking advantage of you."

"Well," Ginny gave me an impish grin, "sometimes after I clean up, I study and do my homework here. Quieter than the dorm."

I laughed. "I'd imagine so. But you're not staying too late and driving back to school when it's dark are you?"

"It's fiiiiiiiiine, Si," she said. "I'm tough."

I sighed.

"Well," I said, "all right. Going home does sound good right now. I have plenty to do, I'm sure. Online clients to respond to, uh, housework, get your payroll figured out for Thursday. I'm sure you'd appreciate that."

I'd said "housework" but I meant "look for my ghost in my house." The rest was true, though.

"I do like getting paid on time," Ginny replied.

"All right," I said. "You've convinced me. Will you stay open a little bit longer, just in case anyone stops by? Then you can finish up and study all you want. Half hour?"

"Sure thing, boss man!" Ginny gave me a sharp salute.

Laughing, we parted ways. I gathered up my things, put my coat and scarf back on, and headed out. Before I knew it, I was in my car and headed back to the house. My mind, for some reason, felt like it was racing as I drove, but I couldn't figure out why. My thoughts were erratic and complex. What I even wanted to think about eluded me. Every time I tried to pin down one thought, it flittered away, replaced by another random thought.

Pushing my mind clear, I was approaching my driveway before I knew it. Finding Danny's truck outside my house and him sitting in one of the chairs on my porch did not surprise me one bit. I took my time parking and getting out of the car, not caring how long Danny sat hunched over, holding his coat tightly around himself on my porch.

If he was that cold, he should have stayed in his truck with the heater on.

"Figured you'd be here," I said calmly as I approached the porch.

"Regular Sherlock Holmes," Danny mumbled.

I went straight to the front door and unlocked it, then went inside without another word. Danny entered a few seconds behind me. I put away my coat and scarf and headed to the kitchen, ignoring Danny. His footsteps through the house behind me let me know he was following.

After I grabbed a diet soda from the fridge, I turned to find him standing right behind me. I nearly jumped at his closeness, but I managed to stay planted. Popping the tab of the can, I brought it to my lips and took a long swallow as I stared at him.

"You were at her funeral," Danny said.

"Get out," I replied.

"That's how you knew what she was buried in," Danny continued, ignoring me. "That's the only way you could know."

I stared at him for a moment, took another sip of my drink. Proving to Danny that I was not a fraud was not even in the top one hundred things on my agenda. However, I was angry.

"Didn't your grandmother die while we were in college?" I asked.

"Yes," Danny said. "So?"

"I went to college in California," I said. "Your grandmother died in the middle of February. I was across the country when you came home for the funeral. Or do you not remember calling me? Crying to me from nearly two thousand miles away? How could I have seen what she looked like in her casket, Danny?"

He chewed at his lip, averting his eyes.

"I offered to come home to be with you for a few days, but you insisted that I don't disrupt my studies. Remember?"

Danny finally looked back at me.

"Then why won't you actually summon my dad?" he asked, quietly.

"He never shows up when I try to summon him for your mother," I said. "I've told you that. I can't force ghosts to do things. They're not compelled to answer me. I've told you this."

"But why wouldn't he show up?" His eyes were pleading with me for answers. "Why? I was even there today."

I shrugged. "I don't have the answers you want, Danny. Your father will or won't show up as he wishes. Just like every other ghost. That's all I can tell you."

Danny threw his hands up and marched out of the kitchen. I took another sip of my drink as I stood there in the kitchen. When I didn't hear the front door open and shut, I sighed and headed to the living room. I found Danny sitting on the sofa, his head in his hands. I leaned against the doorjamb and stared at him, holding my half-empty can of soda.

"What do you want from me?" I asked. "I mean, I know what you *usually* want when you show up here. But that's not what's on your mind tonight."

Danny rubbed his face with the palm of his hands before finally looking up at me. His eyes were red, but no tears had been shed yet.

"I want you to stop giving my mother hope."

"I don't give her hope," I said. "I've told her time and time again he's not going to show up, but she keeps insisting I try. Why she does it is her business. Not yours and not mine."

Danny considered me for a moment.

"Fine."

"Fine," I replied and necked the rest of the soda.

I gasped and burped.

"Now what?" I asked.

"What do you mean?"

"Is that all the questions you had?"

"I guess. Yeah," Danny said. "You can't really tell me anything else. Or won't. Or can't. Jeez, I don't even know with you anymore."

"Well," I said, gesturing vaguely, "see yourself out. You got—or didn't get—what you came for."

I turned to go back into the kitchen, but Danny was suddenly behind me, his hands on my shoulders. Tensing under his grip, I did all I could to not physically react too obviously.

"You don't want me to stay longer?" he murmured, moving his mouth close to my neck.

For a moment, I considered this.

"Go home, Danny," I said. "Leave me be."

"Why, though?" Danny kissed my neck.

I jerked away and stepped back to look at him.

"Your mother didn't ask you to sit in on the session today," I said. "We both know it. You came to try and prove me a fraud. In fact, I think that's where everything was going to go...until I planted a seed of doubt in your head by telling you *exactly* what your grandmother was buried in. And you know I'd have no way of knowing if I couldn't see ghosts."

Danny's jaw clenched and flexed as he stared at me.

"So," I said, "you've got what you needed. Go home. Drive back up to Dubuque. I'm sure you've been leaving all of your work to your foremen lately. You're always down here. Go take care of your actual business and stay out of mine."

"You don't mean that."

"I do," I said, pointing at the door. "Go."

Danny considered me for a moment, his cheeks going red.

"For how long?" he asked. "How long do you want me to stay out of your business?"

"I'll let you know."

Danny reddened, but he said nothing. He opened his mouth to argue, but he quickly shut it. Finally, he gave up and turned to leave. He ripped the front door open and turned to look at me. His mouth opened again, but his jaw just ended up hanging there briefly before it was shut again. He breezed out the door, closing it behind him.

I stood in the living room, crunching the can in my hand as I listened to the footsteps on the gravel outside. Then the sound of a truck door opening and closing. I refused to dash out the door and stop him. Then his truck started up, he revved the engine, and I heard him turning his truck to leave. I forced myself to stay in spot there in the living room, waiting until the sound of his truck dissipated down the driveway.

Once I was certain he was gone, I angrily threw the crushed can into the kitchen, hearing it clattered against the cabinet. Then I stomped over to the sofa and threw myself into it, mirroring Danny's position from before, my head in my hands. Mirroring his previous actions, I rubbed my palms into my eyes, growling with frustration as I dropped my hands to my lap and stared out at nothing.

Though I always did my best to not make it my first thought every time I was in my house, my mind went to the ghost. It was hiding somewhere in the house. Ghosts, as most people who believe in them know, are often unseen by the world around them. However, many mediums, such as myself, can see them everywhere. Even with the abilities I possess, ghosts can hide themselves from me quite well if they so choose.

Most ghosts don't expend their time or energy hiding, though. Humans already can't see them. They're dead. Nothing can hurt them to the point of destroying them that I know of; they can hurt temporarily and be trapped. So, why bother hiding? Though most ghosts can't be trapped forever. They eventually will find a way out of anything, but traps can last a very long time if done well.

Houses, protected from ghosts, can keep them out indefinitely. Trapping ghosts out of something is much more effective than trapping them in something. Ghosts want to get out and roam. They don't want to find their way inside a place they may not be able to get out of again. It's why protected houses generally stay safe for long periods of time. Generations.

"So," I said out loud as I stared and my eyes glazed over, "who trapped you?"

Obviously, the ghost didn't saunter in from the kitchen with a can of beer, ready to talk.

"And why?"

I thought about this for what seemed like forever.

"How long were you trapped?" I thought out loud once more.

It occurred to me that a ghost would have no reason to want to hide from me in my own house. Unless it was afraid I'd put it back in the box. It would only be afraid enough to hide itself from me for that reason if it had been in the box long enough to have grown to hate it.

How long were you in there? I thought.

My eyes landed on the teal cupboard sitting alongside the opposite wall.

Months?

A niggling thought entered my head. My vision unblurred and I rose from the sofa like a robot, thoughts swirling through my head. On autopilot, I went to the front door, shrugged my coat and scarf on, and headed out.

CHAPTER 15

A lot of things I am, but a fool is not one. Even in a small town with so few people living in it, it's best to be safe. At night, things are even more noticeable to the citizens of Sage Grove. Due to the low population, one open business, and no real foot traffic through town at night, a person wandering downtown at night sticks out like a sore thumb. Unless you're at the Wash-A-Teria or the Gas & Go, there's really no point in being in the main part of town at night.

Anyone out that late in the area is obviously unhoused, or up to trouble. Either thing is a potential call to the county police. So, I had parked my car at The Lunch Counter and went inside to wait until it was fully dark. No one would think it too odd seeing my car at the diner at night. They'd just assume I was doing paperwork or prepping for the next day. It was my business, so I had every right to be there, even at night.

When night came and the town grew dark as a tomb, I switched off the lights in The Lunch Counter and left, locking the door tightly behind me. However, I didn't climb back into my car and go home. I walked along the old shuttered buildings that used to house businesses, keeping to the shadows.

Every now and then, I'd duck under an awning and wait. I'd look around and make sure no one was out for a nightly walk or heading to the laundromat or gas station. Though I wasn't doing anything crazy, the legality of my purpose was firmly on the side of not.

It took some doing, going slow and cautiously, but I finally found myself in the shadow of an awning across from The Eternity Inn. I stood there for a while, as the night grew darker, and stared up at the old two-story Victorian. No longer white, but weathered gray by age, the elements, and lack of care, it looked spooky. The windows were all boarded tightly on the front, so I had to assume they were everywhere else on the building.

With the front door boards still tightly in place, I had to assume that every other entrance had gotten the same treatment when it had been shuttered. At first glance, the job of closing it up had been a good job. Not a board out of place. Since I had no other option, I ducked out of the shadows and dashed across the street after a quick glance around.

Within two seconds, I was across the street and hiding in the shadows alongside the inn. I took a second to collect myself and take a few steadying breaths, then I crept along the side of the building, checking the windows, as I made my way to the back. All of the windows on the left side of the Victorian were boarded up, same as the front. I'd make my way around the entire building, checking every entrance before I gave up.

At the rear of the building, I found the back entrance boarded as tightly, if not more so than the front. Seeing the boards screwed into the jamb made my heart sink. It seemed pointless to go around and check the last side of the inn. However, I knew that I'd never get a good night's rest if I didn't at least check.

Creeping back down the steps from the backdoor, I was determined to finish checking the windows when my eyes landed on a curious sight. The bulkhead doors leading into the basement. The Eternity Inn having bulkhead doors, and a cellar, wasn't what gave me pause. The fact that it was fall and not a single leaf, vine, or other detritus was on them did.

The Eternity Inn had been closed up for months. No one had been to the inn—to my knowledge—since the county had shuttered it for the Milners. In a few months, surely the doors would be littered with anything and everything blown around by the wind. Furthermore, there wasn't a chain or lock that I could see on the doors.

Hoping against hope, I went over to the bulkhead doors and grabbed the handle. I stopped myself, realizing that even if I lucked out, another problem might present itself. Even if the inn had a cellar and the bulkhead doors to walk into the cellar from the outside, I wasn't certain it had access to the main building. The cellar could simply be a shelter or used solely for storage.

Another problem was the condition of the doors. If I opened them after months—or longer—of not being used, they might creak. Maybe creak loudly enough to draw attention from people living nearby. Knowing without looking that the windows on the other side of the building were surely boarded up, I swallowed my fear and pulled at the handle.

Though not as loud as I'd feared, the door did creak a bit, though it came up easily. I gently tilted it until it was laying on the ground and then stood to stare down at the steps and the black hole into which they led. I pulled my phone out and took off down the stairs, not wanting to turn the flashlight on my phone on until I was inside

Once my head was below the bulkhead doors, I stopped and turned on my flashlight. Not powerful enough to illuminate an entire cellar, the flashlight still gave me enough illumination to see where I was going. Treading lightly, I made my way down the old wooden steps, cringing and wincing at every creak and crack.

Safely at the bottom, I turned and looked at the stairs I'd come down, wondering how they hadn't collapsed on me. Hopefully, on my way out, I wouldn't have any issues. Pushing the thought away that I might have trapped myself in a cellar with no real exit, I began to turn to have a look around.

Before I could focus my attention elsewhere, something on the stairs caught my eye. How I had noticed it in such low light, I wasn't sure, but something was etched into the step of each stair. Drawing closer, I leaned down to look at the steps. Starting from the bottom step, I worked my way up a few, looking closely at each.

Inconsistent etches—or gouge marks—were in each step. They were in pairs. One on the left and one on the right, each pair on each step approximately three feet apart. Frowning, I shut off the flashlight and walked back up the stairs. They creaked and groaned but held. I didn't completely leave the basement, but I looked out far enough to examine the ground in front of the bulkhead doors.

Impressions in the soft ground. Something had sat—or dropped—there. Fairly recently. They weren't deep enough that a good rain wouldn't have made them invisible. Frowning, I turned back around and went back down the steps. Back at the base of the stairs, I went back to my flashlight and my perusal of the rest of the cellar.

Surprisingly, it appeared to have been used for cold food storage at some point, though all of the shelves were now, obviously, bare. However, a staircase across the twelve-by-ten room led upwards. A smile came to my face as I hoped that those stairs were also in usable condition.

More creaking and groaning echoed in the basement, but I found that the staircase on the other side of the room still functioned. When my flashlight shone on the door at the top of the stairs, I took a deep breath, hoping that the interior doors had not been locked or nailed shut. A quick twist of the knob and a shove proved that I was in luck.

Stale, dusty air greeted my nostrils as I stepped into the kitchen of the inn. As though frozen in time, it looked as though nothing had been damaged or touched since it had been shut off from the world. Surely, the layer of dust on everything had not been there before, but everything else looked to be in tip-top shape.

The main floor was not of interest to me, but I knew I had to move cautiously through the inn. Even though it wasn't closed off due to its condition, there was no telling what type of water damage could have occurred in the months since. I had no knowledge of how well it had been kept up before its closing, either. Caution was paramount.

Out of the kitchen and down a long hallway, I found reception. A dining room was across the way, with a stairway splitting the two. Which was exactly what I was looking for when I came to the inn. Access to the second floor of The Eternity Inn.

With the flashlight guiding me, I eased up the stairs, finding it solid and mostly quiet. A slight creak and groan here and there, but nothing like the basement steps. The upstairs hallway, with its long runner carpet running from one end to the other, was also in good condition. Dark as midnight due to the lack of outside light, my flashlight barely allowed me to see ten feet in front of my face.

Not wanting to be in the building any longer than necessary, I walked down the long hallway lined with doors. Each door provided access to one of the rooms that were once rented out by the night. Methodically, I went from door to door as I made my way down the hall, popping each one open and shining my light inside each.

First door on the right. First door on the left. On and on down the hall. By the time I got to the fourth door on the right, I'd about given up. Few doors remained to check. However, when I popped the door open, and shone my light inside, the bed, dresser, and small wingback chair coming into view, I stopped. It wasn't the furniture that caught my attention so much as the teal color of the walls.

I glanced up and down the hall, then ducked inside the room. Walking across the room, I took in the furniture in view, noticing two doors on the wall to my right that most likely went to a closet and an en suite. Both had been nailed shut. However, as I took in the room, I realized that what I'd expected to find—or not find—was not apparent.

Finally, after several moments of staring at the room, I sighed and lowered the flashlight. Shaking my head and chuckling at my stupidity at having such a wild idea, I gave up. I turned around, intending to leave The Eternity Inn for good. However, when I turned, raising the flashlight as I did, the long wall alongside the open door caught my eye.

The dark chestnut wainscoting and chair rail were dusty, but pristine. As was the teal wallpaper above it that led all the way up to the white ceiling. On the wall, further way from the door was a picture, some painting that I couldn't make out unless I was willing to dust it off. It was of no interest to me, though. What interested me wasn't what was there—it was what wasn't there.

The three foot wide, six-foot-tall shadow on the wall made me cock my head to the side. Something large had been sitting there. Something that most likely matched the room.

Something teal.

Before I had much time to really consider things, movement at the door caught my eye. Spinning on my heels, I shone my flashlight at the door. A face was staring at me from around the doorjamb. Startled by the sudden appearance of the person, I jumped, nearly dropping the flashlight. The man dashed away, but not before I caught the flutter of his cardigan in the open doorway.

"Wait!" I barked. "Crap!"

I dashed from the from the room and out into the hall. Footsteps on the stairs, rushing away, were already reaching my ears. I tore down the hallway with reckless abandon, the beam of the flashlight bobbling all around me, cutting frantic shadows on the walls of the hallway.

Leaping down the stairs, two at a time, I rushed down to the first floor of the inn. Footsteps were hammering into the kitchen, and I followed them. In the kitchen, I could hear footsteps on the stairs into the cellar. By the time I got to the stairs and down them, I could see the rectangle of light at the top of the exit to the cellar from the bullhead door across the room. The flutter of a cardigan was briefly visible, then gone.

I raced across the cellar and up the steps, ignoring the stairs protests, and practically fell into the backyard of the inn. Leaping up, I looked around frantically, but found nothing. Just the whistle of the wind. My hair fluttered in the wind, but all was silent.

Gary was gone.

CHAPTER 16

"I know that it's eat this or maybe nothing," Ginny was saying, "but I still feel bad scooping this up. Even for the folks at the camp."

I was methodically packing a bag for Sal in advance of her arrival, barely listening to Ginny talk. My mind was on the previous night's events. Even though I liked to be present in most aspects of my life, I couldn't get myself to focus. Thoughts kept swirling around my brain, invading every moment of every task I took on at the diner.

After my evening prowl into The Eternity Inn, I had gone home, made sure everything was locked up tight, and checked all the silver pieces in the corners of doors and windows. Then I'd cleaned up, crawled under the covers, and fell into a fitful sleep. When I woke up, my mind began racing with thoughts.

Breakfast went by in a flash I was so unfocused on my toast and coffee. I was barely able to remember my morning shower, getting dressed, and getting in my car to go to work. How I arrived at The Lunch Counter without running off the road was incredible. The fact that I'd been quiet all morning, lost in thought, and Ginny hadn't mentioned, it was a miracle.

"I mean, tuna noodle casserole, Si?" Ginny said.

Her cooking spoon squished and squelched in the dishes as she served up portions into plastic to-go containers.

"They're already homeless. Must we continue to punish them with *tuna noodle casserole*?"

I snapped another lid on another full container of the concoction as I made a humming sound with my throat.

Ginny said nothing, but she stopped talking, which let me know she had gotten the hint. I wasn't in the mood, or capable, of carrying on a decent conversation. I could feel the clock ticking until the moment she asked me what was wrong, but I was delaying it for as long as possible. Of course, my answer would be that I slept poorly, had a crick in my neck, had a lot of work with my website, the usual excuses I made when I was in a mood. And she'd pretend to believe it.

Then I'd come in the next day, right as rain, and all would be forgotten and forgiven.

I found myself glancing at the front window every few minutes. The ghost that had been following me was staring through the front window, unmoving. Floating in the air outside, its eyes framed by the O in the diner's name painted on the window, it refused to move. It was going to spend all day watching me as I worked. Until I left to go home for the day, I knew it would be there, watching me.

"Okay," Ginny finally said, "you've been ho-humming all morning long. Ignoring me. What's up, Si?"

"I didn't—"

"Sleep well," Ginny finished for me, drawing my attention from the window.

When I turned to look at her, her arms were folded over her chest, the cooking spoon still gripped in one hand. The sauce from the casserole decorated the spoon, but fortunately, it was clean enough that nothing was dripping off of it.

"Sorry," I said automatically.

Ginny's brow rose, crinkling her forehead.

"Are you okay?" she asked, going back to scooping up portions of the casserole. "Is the smell coming off this making you sick, too?"

Somehow, I managed to a chuckle.

"It's just tuna," I said. "It doesn't smell bad. We're in the Midwest. Stop acting so fancy."

Ginny gave a genuine laugh. I shot a look at the window to find the ghost was still staring at me. I don't know why I would have expected anything different. Once a ghost decides you're a target, they tend to stick around them as much as they can. Travelers are the worst. Especially when they want something from you.

"This isn't about Victor Grimm is it?" Ginny asked. "The article?"

I looked at her.

"In the Grove Gossip?" Ginny asked. "Them mentioning his upcoming appearance in Dubuque and the ticket sales and all that?"

I snorted. "I didn't know the Grove Gossip was still putting out...*flyers?*"

"Papers."

"Sure," I said. "If you want to call the one sheet of postings about local happenings a *paper*. I didn't know they mentioned him."

She nodded. "He's got that show coming up in Dubuque next month. Thought maybe you—"

I waved her off. "I don't care about Victor Grimm. He's a fraud anyway."

"A fraud who rakes in the dough," Ginny said. "Heard he might be getting a T.V. show or something."

I ignored her.

"I guess I'm just not feeling great," I said.

I faked a small cough into the crook of my elbow.

"Felt a little down when I went to sleep last night. Probably just an allergy or sinus thing. Worn down."

"You better not be getting sick!" Ginny wailed as she portioned out the casserole. "I've got so many tests this week that I cannot miss!"

"I'm not sick."

"How can you be so sure?"

"I'm not running a fever," I said, chuckling. "It's just a sinus or allergy thing. You know? Autumn. Once all the trees have shed their leaves and winter settles in, I won't have a single sniffle until Spring."

"True," Ginny said.

"That's twenty," I said, snapping the last lid on a to-go tub.

I put the last stack in the bag for Sal, folded the top, and pushed it to the side. Ginny already had most of the casseroles we'd baked off portioned out and in containers, so I went up and down the table where she'd laid them out, snapping on the lids. Everyone that came into The Lunch Counter could get a portion or two and heat them up at home. Or eat them cold. Whatever tickled their fancy—we weren't the food police.

"I wish we had more to offer today," Ginny lamented.

"I know," I said. "Fresh groceries in the morning. But you know we have to use everything up. Spoilage doesn't look good here. We can't waste anything. Tuna noodle casserole it was."

"I know, I know," she said. "It just feels cruel."

I laughed and went around the counter to sit down on one of the stools, groaning as I lowered myself. Ginny glanced at me over her shoulder, but said nothing. Instead, she finished dishing out the rest of the casserole from the pans and put the lids on the last few to-go containers. Whoever came in within the next hour would get a tub or two. Anything still sitting out after an hour would be put in the fridge for another time.

Or Ginny could take the leftovers to the dorm and pass them out to her friends so it wouldn't go to waste. If she didn't think it would offend them too much. Though she had plenty of thoughts about the casserole, I had a feeling her poor college dormmates who had been living on instant noodles for weeks or months would probably be glad to have the food. I was opening my mouth to give her my suggestion when a cold gust of air rolled through the diner.

I spun on the stool, the vinyl crackling under me and the turn mechanism creaking as I did. The front door was wide open and Sal was rushing inside, pushing the door shut against the wind that was trying to force its way inside. Once the door was closed and she turned to face me, I couldn't help but grin at her wind-rustled hair and the scarf that had flapped up to cover most of her face.

Shaking with cold, she reached up and peeled the scarf from her face. Her skirt had ridden up, but fortunately not so far to be indecent, and her coat look insufficient for the coming weather, but other than that and her hair, she looked unbothered. She beamed upon seeing me and rushed over to the counter.

With Ginny still distracted behind the counter, Sal leaned down to whisper to me.

"*Doc Stephens' old place has been a boon,*" she murmured. "*We stay plenty warm there at night. Thank you, Si. And give our thanks to Caleb.*"

I nodded as she quickly straightened up. Ginny turned around as Sal straightened and gave her a smile.

"Usual order, I'm afraid," she said to my partner before glancing at me. "I don't have a lot to offer today."

"Keep it," I waved her off as I leaned an elbow on the counter. "With winter coming I'm sure everyone could use some socks or whatever you can manage."

Sal got rosy cheeked but said nothing. She gave me a polite nod of thanks and turned her attention back to Ginny.

"Si got you all bagged up already," Ginny said. "This is on him. It's tuna noodle casserole. I told him it was cruel to do to the folks in town who come in for their lunch, but he's evil. You know how he is."

Sal patted my back jovially and laughed at Ginny's comments.

"Everyone in the camp will be glad to have it," she said. "You won't hear one complaint from us."

"We have another delivery tomorrow," I said. "Tomorrow's menu will be much better."

"No complaints." Sal repeated herself.

Ginny retrieved the bag from the prep table and set it on the counter before reaching for the tie of her apron.

"Gotta hit the toilet," she said. "I'll be back."

"Aim true," I quipped.

Ginny rolled her eyes and disappeared into the back. Sal drew the bag from the counter, cradling it in her arm so that the heft wouldn't cause it to break. She looked to the door to the back where Ginny disappeared, waited a second, then turned her attention to me.

"Have you had a chance to...you know?" she asked in a hushed tone.

"I'm asking around." I gave a vague response. "I'll let you know if I hear anything or think of anything else."

Sal gave me an apologetic, sad smile.

"I know you have a lot going on, Si," she said. "It was a big ask. I know you'll get to it when you get to it."

Nodding, I said, "Maybe if I talked to Gary it would help? Have you seen him around? He hasn't popped in today."

Hoping my expression was neutral, I sat there innocently and awaited Sal's response. Instead of immediately responding, she looked towards the window and chewed at her lip, deep in thought. I didn't rush her, afraid I'd appear suspicious. There was one thing the unhoused population of Sage Grove hated—people treating them suspiciously.

"I'm worried about that, too," she said. "I haven't seen him in two days."

"Oh?"

She looked at me and frowned, though she wasn't really looking at me, but through me.

"He took off the other night. Didn't say anything to anyone. Hasn't been back," Sal explained. "I've checked with everyone, but no one has heard anything. I hope he didn't take off to hell knows where to try and find Marcella. Before you know it, we'll all be disappearing."

I gave her an empathetic look and reached up to pat her shoulder.

"I'm sure he'll turn back up soon, Sal," I said, reassuring her. "You know Gary."

She nodded.

"I do know Gary," she said with a chuckle. "He wanders off sometimes. This isn't the longest he's been gone."

"With Marcella missing it probably just makes him being gone seem worse this time," I said.

She gave me a look that told me she agreed. She wiggled her arm holding the bag at me and headed to the door.

"Thanks, Si," she said as she reached for the handle. "For the food. Gary. Doc Stephens."

Bowing my head, I said nothing, and she disappeared out the door, an icy blast of wind replacing her. My eyes shifted to the window and I watched Sal walked down the sidewalk, right through the ghost, shivering as she passed through, though taking no other notice of it. My eyes went back to the ghost and I stared into its eyes.

"She left already?" Ginny asked.

Startled, I nearly fell from the stool. When I whipped around to look at her, she was grinning evilly and tying her apron string back around her waist. A thought that I'd been trying to pin down all morning entered my head and I righted myself on the stool.

"I forgot to ask Sal," I said calmly, "but did she ever mention that girl's last name? Marcella's?"

Ginny turned up the corner of her mouth, deep in thought as she began to gather up the cooking supplies to take to the sink. Finally, she perked up and turned to me.

"Washington," Ginny said. "Marcella Washington. Of course, you never know with the camp folk. The name they go by might not be the one on record with the government."

I nodded, standing from the stool.

"Do you think you can finish up today again?" I asked.

Ginny growled at me, her mouth twisting up in a frown.

"You can pick the menu tomorrow," I said.

She brightened. "Deal!"

Laughing, I headed to the door. I shrugged on my coat and scarf and checked to make sure my keys, wallet, and phone were still in my pockets.

"You're a peach!" I shot over my shoulder to Ginny and breezed out the front door.

Practically leaping into my car, I buckled in and pulled out from in front of the diner. A quick minute later, I was in the

Gas & Go, buying an energy drink. I made sure to thank Caleb on behalf of the camp folks for the tip about Doc Stephens' place, and left, cracking the can open as I slid back into the car.

I was no fool. At least not as big a fool as I could have been. I knew exactly where to find Marcella. But now, with a few pieces of the puzzle falling into place in my brain, and her full name, I knew what could be done. I chugged the drink as I made my way home, not bothering to abide the laws of the road. County officers rarely patrolled the streets from town out to my house.

By the time I was parking in the driveway in front of my house, I was tossing the empty can into the back floorboard. I didn't bother locking my car as I leapt out and headed into the house. My coat and scarf got put on the coat rack inside and I made my way into the bedroom.

In my bedroom, I retrieved the humidifier from the closet and dug around until I found my bundle of sage. I made a trip to the kitchen and filled the humidifier up with water and then took it and placed it on the coffee table in the living room. It took a while, digging around in the chest of supplies I had out in the atrium, but I finally found the sage essential oil and an old cigarette lighter I kept on hand. Back in the living room, I deposited a few teaspoons of the liquid into the water in the humidifier.

Throwing myself down on the sofa, I heaved out a breath, laying the sage bundle on the coffee table. The sun was halfway to the horizon outside after what seemed like forever, but I continued to wait, playing a game on my phone as the minutes ticked by. My stomach grumbled, so I made a sandwich with a side of chips and had a quick bite in the kitchen before returning to my spot on the sofa in the living room.

Night seemed to take forever to arrive, especially with watching the clock and not much else. However, when the sun dipped below the horizon, and the light ceased to peek through the blinds in the living room, the time had come. I rose from the sofa and looked around cautiously. Knowing that there was no turning back, not if I wanted to solve more than one problem, I opened my mouth to speak.

"Marcella Washington!"

CHAPTER 17

"I'm Silas Erie," I continued. "Medium, lifeline to the dead, communicator with souls. I have a question from your friend. Unfinished business you have on this earth. I summon you!"

Typically, summoning a ghost, if you're an adept or expert medium, everything except the ghost's name is theater. However, even though I've been summoning ghosts for nearly fifteen years—since right before puberty got its fangs in me— I find the theater helpful. It compels the ghosts, it seems. Makes them feel as though they are dealing with an authority they should not refuse.

Ghosts who do not spend much time around other ghosts have no idea that there is no authority in the afterlife. At least none that I've witnessed. No one is going to arrest a ghost, take it to ghost court, and put it on ghost trial. Death is final. There are no further repercussions for the dead. If they refuse to answer a medium, well, what's the worst that could happen to them?

Super death?

No such thing.

I stood in the living room, waiting for the ghost to show itself. If it was Marcella, she should be compelled to slither out of whatever hidey-hole she'd found and materialize for me. If I was wrong, then I'd wasted all of my time.

I was about to open my mouth to summon the ghost once more when I felt a coolness emanating from the hallway.

Lowering myself to the sofa, I sat back, waiting for the ghost to make up its mind. Five minutes ticked by like hours as the cool breeze silently spread through the living room. Finally, after what seemed like an eternity, the blueish-gray glow of a materializing ghost trickled from the hallway.

It was just a slight shimmer in the air at first, the ghost, but as I waited and stared at the hallway opening, the image became clearer. Feet, a few inches off the ground, transparent and glowing, began to materialize, then jeans covered legs, hips, abdomen, torso, arms, and then a head.

The ghost shimmering in the door to the hallway was a thin woman who had seen her share of hunger. Beautiful, even in her gauntness, with a long mane of dark hair, gangly limbs, and impossibly small waist. Wracking my brain, I plucked a few memories out. Marcella Washington, one of the folks from the camp, who I had seen a handful of times was standing before me. I was certain of it.

I'd only seen her a few times. At the Gas & Go begging for change or food. Outside the Wash-A-Teria. Walking with the folks from the camp. Ducking around corners when folks from town who were not homeless appeared to be bothered by her presence. She was one of the folks from camp most sensitive to the unkindness of those more fortunate, no matter how much. She didn't trust anyone in town. Except a man that might have money to spare.

"Were you Marcella Washington?"

The ghost said nothing, only a low moan escaped her mouth when her jaw creaked open. She stared at me with haunted eyes that still somehow had a sparkle to them. Floating before me in my own living room, she examined me carefully, drawing no closer than a foot from the hallway door.

"Are you aware you're dead?" I asked.

Another moan escaped her mouth, which had not closed since the first moan.

Great.

Not even a Screamer. A Moaner. I'd have to update my records about the many different kinds of ghosts.

"You're new dead," I said aloud, though I wasn't really talking to Marcella. "Haven't talked to anyone since you died."

I stared through, not at the ghost. Seconds ticked by.

"If you understand me," I said, looking into her eyes finally, "moan twice."

The ghost stared at me long enough to make me think it was hopeless, but after that pause, two moans escaped her mouth. I couldn't help but smile.

"Good," I said. "Were you Marcella Washington? One moan for 'no' and two for 'yes', please."

A moan came, but not a second. Confused, I cocked my head to the side. I wasn't great with names, and I didn't go around introducing myself to people willy-nilly, but I remembered this woman. I remembered seeing her with the camp folks. With Gary.

This was Marcella Washington. I was sure of it.

A thought occurred to me and I shook my head, realizing what an idiot I'd been.

"*Are* you Marcella Washington?" I asked.

The ghost moaned twice.

The freshly dead don't like the past tense.

"Are you aware you are dead?"

One moan.

I sighed.

"Well," I said, "I regret to inform you that you *were* Marcella Washington. And you *are* dead. You're a ghost. I'm a medium. You're trapped in my house and I've summoned you."

One moan.

"I have no reason to lie," I said.

Another moan. Frantic.

"Calm down," I said. "I can prove it to you."

A single moan, but less frantic. Somehow, this moan sounded skeptical. Scared.

"But I'll need to trap you in a box again," I said.

Another scared moan came from Marcella's ghost and she began to drift backward.

"Wait," I said firmly, and Marcella stopped, staring daggers at me.

She moaned once more.

"Marcella Washington," I said, "I have two options. I dislike one, and I hate the other. You'll feel the same about them."

She stared at me but no moan came forth.

"You can let me trap you and take out of this house and prove to you that you are, indeed, a ghost," I said, "or I have one other option."

I nodded at the humidifier on the table and the bundle of sage.

"I will turn this on and fill this house with mist imbued with sage oil. I will burn this sage bundle and waft the smoke into every crevice of this house. You will have nowhere to turn. Nowhere to run. And it will hurt. Sage and silver hurt ghosts. I don't want to hurt you. But to get you out of my house, I will do it. However, I will let you decide if you want to go willingly and painlessly by being trapped, or if you want me to go this the hard way."

She moaned once but didn't move.

"I'm a nice person," I said. "I don't like hurting anyone. But this is my house and you are not welcome and do not belong here. I will remove you, one way or another."

Marcella stared at me, then her eyes shot to the table.

"If you make this difficult, I will simply remove you from this house and not help you any further," I said. "If you cooperate, I will prove to you that you are a ghost and help you."

She said nothing; didn't move.

"Please don't make me be a bad person," I said, pleading. "Let me trap you. Prove to you that you are a ghost. And then I will set you free. I will not keep you trapped for a long time like you were in the cupboard."

She looked back to me.

"I promise."

It seemed like forever before Marcella reacted.

Two moans emanated from that gaping mouth.

CHAPTER 18

When I arrived in town, the wooden box and hammer in the passenger seat beside me, I didn't park by The Lunch Counter. I drove through town, driving at a crawl, making sure that I drove by every alleyway and side street. Drove by each abandoned building, including Doc Stephens' old place. I stopped and got an energy drink from the Gas & Go and chatted with Caleb for a moment before getting back in my car.

After being certain I'd driven every inch of the main part of town, I drove back down to the diner. I went inside and put the energy drink in the fridge for the following morning and went back to the car. Instead of getting in and driving off, I opened the passenger door and retrieved the wooden box. Though I wasn't certain I was right, niggling doubts tugged at the corner of my brain.

Ignoring all of those thoughts, I took the box under my arm, tucked the hammer into a belt loop, and locked my car. I didn't stick to the shadows or creep around like I had the night before. A beeline was cut from the diner to The Eternity Inn. Upon approaching the old, off-white Victorian, I walked around the back, and slung the bulkhead door to the cellar open. I didn't worry about the creak or the "thump" the door made against the ground.

Drawing attention to my presence wasn't a concern.

The stairs creaked and groaned as I descended into the black hole of the cellar, guided only by the weak beam of my phone flashlight. But as they had the night before, the stairs held true. Now that I knew the layout of the place, I made my way across the cellar and up the old, yet reliable stairs into the kitchen of the inn.

A few moments later and I was climbing the stairs to the second floor. I didn't have to guess which room was important when I got into the upstairs hallway. I went straight to the door to the teal room and ducked inside. I looked around, my eye stopping on the shadow on the wall where the cupboard once stood, then went about doing the job I'd come to do.

In the center of the room, I set the green sage-ash painted wood box with inlaid silver at every corner. Kneeling in front of it, my fingers reached for the clasp. When I flipped it up, I expected a woosh of air and for Marcella's ghost to fly out frantically. Instead, I only felt a cold presence and found myself staring into the blueish-gray shimmer of Marcella's form packed into the box like sardines.

"We're here," I said. "I told you I wouldn't keep you trapped long."

Long.

What is long to a ghost? When you've lived years as a human and then find yourself facing eternity, what does time even mean? Marcella's time in the box could have felt like an instant or an eternity to her.

"You can come out," I said gently. "I won't trap you again."

A pair of transparent shimmery eyes stared out from the blob of ghost parts in the box, examining me.

"I promise."

Slowly, like a mist made of death, Marcella's ghost leaked from the box, bit by bit, as she had done when she materialized at my house. I waited patiently as she extracted herself from the confines of box and materialized in her ghostly form before me. Once I was satisfied that she was completely out of the box, and that I was keeping none of her inside, I shut and latched it again.

When she didn't welp or moan, I knew that she had truly, fully extracted herself.

I stood, leaving the box in place for the moment, and faced Marcella Washington.

"Still not talking?" I asked, though I knew it would be pointless.

One moan sounded.

I nodded, gravely.

"Do you know what happens to someone when they die, Marcella?" I asked softly.

She said nothing, didn't moan, but still stared at me as if I was the crazy person in the equation. I sighed and rubbed my hands on the thighs of my pants.

"Generally," I say, "the experience is traumatic. As you can imagine. As you may remember, given enough time living...*unliving*...outside of a box. They usually find a place to hide. Gather their thoughts, examine what they are feeling and what has happened to them. If they even understand what has happened."

The ghost stared, her mouth agape.

"Some people know immediately that they are dead. Some don't," I added. "Either way, they know something is wrong, so they look for safety, just as they would if they were still alive. Human."

Two moans escaped the ghost. At least I knew she was following what I was saying.

"Ghosts are attracted to shimmery things immediately," I said. "I don't know if it's because they are suddenly shimmery and something...primal...attracts them to things that shimmer. I'll figure it out one day, maybe. Or I'll figure it out when it's my turn to be a ghost. Either way, silver attracts the freshly dead. Even if it is dangerous to them. They all learn one way or another to avoid things that shimmer—except other ghosts."

Marcella stared at me, floating a few inches from the ground, her feet at an angle so that her toes pointed straight down at the floor.

"That's why it gets harder to trap a ghost the longer they've been dead. They learn what to avoid. Fresh ghosts…well, they figure things out eventually. They learn the hard way or start talking to other ghosts. Or that primal thing makes their instincts kick in. It's why you hid from me in the house. You'd already been trapped once. Figured it out the hard way. Though you've still refused to acknowledge your death."

She moaned twice.

"I believe you didn't get into that cupboard after you died simply because someone asked," I said.

A single moan sounded.

"So," I said, "I think that you died, saw the silver, and rushed towards it. Then someone shut the cupboard, locking you—now a ghost—inside."

She moaned once.

"I promised to prove that," I said with a nod. "If you won't believe me by simply looking down at your…body…then I'll have to show you the proof."

Marcella Washington had a look on her face that she already wanted to believe me as she looked down at her transparent form, but she was too angry at being dead to accept it. With a sigh, I removed the hammer from the belt loop and went over to the closet door that had been nailed shut. Fortunately, only two nails at the top, and three on the side had been roughly nailed into the frame. They popped out easily enough.

Swinging the door wide, I was slightly shocked to find it empty. Marcella moved up behind me to examine the nonexistent evidence in the small closet. Undeterred, I moved over to the bathroom and popped the nails that had been used to seal it shut. This door, unlike the closet, pushed inwards, not out. When I went to open it, even with the nails removed, it resisted. Frowning, I looked around the frame, confused.

Finally, I noticed the problem. Kneeling down, I found some type of material stuffed between the floor and the door itself. I swallowed hard and yanked at the material. It took some doing, but I finally yanked it free, nearly falling onto my backside when it whipped out of the crack.

The smell was immediate and nauseating, though far subtler than I imagined it would be. Enough time does that.

I glanced up at Marcella behind me, then stood. Sighing, I knew that I was about to add trauma to Marcella's list, but nothing else could be done. She had to come to terms with her new existence as a ghost. I grabbed the knob, twisted, and pushed the door once more. This time, it swung freely.

The smell of death whispered into the room, and I immediately reconfigured my scarf to cover my mouth and nose, leaving only my eyes visible. In all actuality, the smell was not that strong, but the smell of death is still unpleasant. I didn't want it to work its way into my sinuses and follow me for days.

Marcella followed me as I entered the bathroom, her ghostly form cold at my back. Inside the white-tiled Art Deco bathroom, there was a toilet, a basin sink with a mirror above it, and an old clawfoot tub with the shower curtain closed around it. I walked over and grabbed the curtain, took a deep breath, and pulled it back.

Marcella Washington—or what I assumed was her—was in the tub. Mostly bones and the clothes she had been wearing—that her ghost was now wearing—she was definitely dead. I stared down at the poor woman's body, blinking a few times, taking in the clothes, the necklace around her neck, and the stringy hair laid out around her skull.

Shaking my head, I stepped aside as Marcella Washington's ghost began to moan. Not once, not twice, but one long, sorrowful moan. There was no way to comfort the dead, especially one who has just found out that they are dead. So, I simply stood there beside her as she stared down at her dead body in the tub and moaned.

As she moaned, I examined Marcella's body with my flashlight, letting it scan her body. I'm no medical examiner, but I could spot a broken clavicle and hyoid bone easily enough. Marcella Washington had probably been struck and strangled. It was probably asking too much that she remembered her killer, but I asked anyway, though I wasn't certain I needed confirmation.

"Do you remember who killed you, Marcella?" I asked.

She kept moaning a while longer, then gave me a single moan.

No.

"Maybe you will one day," I said softly. "Once you've had time."

I turned to her and looked into her eyes that no longer looked angry. She looked sad. Mournful.

"If you ever get your voice," I murmured, "you know where I am. Find me. I'll be happy to talk with you."

Marcella said nothing, but I could tell by the new twinkle in her eye that she understood. She floated there before me for a few moments, bobbing in the air, then she began to back away. When she was nearing the doorway to the bathroom, I spoke again.

"Lots of ghosts in the woods out by my house," I said. "Usually during the day, they keep to themselves. But at night they come out. They can help you. Teach you things. If you want."

Marcella stopped for a moment to consider what I said, then she was zipping away like a mist blowing off the ocean. When she zipped out the bathroom door, she blew right through a dark form. I didn't jump or scream, I simply crooked my head to look around the man to make sure Marcella made her way out of the inn room and disappeared.

Where she was going first, I had no idea. But her justice was done. She was aware she was dead. She'd figure things out eventually. So, once I was certain she was gone, I lifted my phone to shine my flashlight on Gary.

"Were you able to see her?" I asked, calmly.

Gary's eyes, squinting against the beam of light, looked me over.

"Just now?"

Gary said and did nothing for several moments, but finally he shook his head. I lowered the light enough to get it out of his eyes, but kept him illuminated.

"She's in here," I said. "But you know that."

Gary nodded.

I watched him for a moment, considering all things, then made a decision.

"You'll want to go now, Gary," I said. "I'm leaving, too. But I'll have to get an anonymous tip to the county police. You won't want to be here for that. They won't understand."

He stared at me.

"Do you hear me? Do you understand?"

He nodded after a moment. His eyes darted to the tub and a single tear slid down his cheek. Then he looked back at me, gave me a bow of his head, and slunk away, disappearing into the shadows. I watched him leave, creeping out of the room into the upstairs hallway, then waited a few moments.

I turned back to the tub and had another look at what had once been Marcella Washington. A young woman, down on her luck, underfed, homeless, penniless, who died trying to do what she had to do to keep herself alive. Such as her life was. I shook my head and left the bathroom.

Both the living and dead were hard to comprehend. Too literal. Too vague. Too proud. Too violent.

If everyone stopped romanticizing what happens on "the other side," none of them would want to know anything about it. But then I'd be out of a job. Maybe some jobs were too much to deal with, actually.

But there's only one thing I know how to do well enough to keep myself and The Lunch Counter going. It was just getting to be too much to do. I swallowed the bile that was threatening to spew forth as I looked around the inn room. Then I stuck the hammer back into the belt loop of my jeans, bent down and grabbed the box, and headed out of The Eternity Inn.

CHAPTER 19

"They're still over there," Ginny said from her place by the window.

She'd been sneaking peeks out the front window of the diner all morning. The ghost that had been following me was right in front of her face, on the other side of the window, but she had no clue. I had been busy scooping Swedish meatballs, mashed potatoes, and buttery peas into to-go containers while she busied herself being a snoop.

"What?" I said, looking up from the prep table.

"The police," Ginny whispered, as though they could hear us. "They're still over at the inn."

I shrugged, though I knew her attention was elsewhere.

"Could be anything," I said nonchalantly.

"For hours?" Ginny was incredulous. "No. Unless...do you think there's a gas leak we need to be worried about? No. Police don't deal with that. Do they?"

"Have you seen the gas company vehicles?" I asked, slopping more food into containers.

Ginny didn't answer me, but she didn't have to respond. Obviously, I knew the answer.

After leaving The Eternity Inn the night before, I walked over to the Gas & Go. I asked Caleb to call the county police when he was ending his shift in the morning and report that he'd seen someone go into The Eternity Inn. No more. No less. He gave me a nod, asked no questions, and followed my directions. I knew he'd say nothing about me.

I was arriving at The Lunch Counter when the police finally came and bothered to check it out. I let Ginny get away with snooping all morning, feeding me information as the cops worked. At first, I was afraid that they would see the boarded-up front door and windows and simply ignore the tip. However, they'd found the bulkhead doors I'd left open at the back of the inn and investigated further. Within twenty minutes of the first cop car showing up, three more arrived, along with an ambulance and fire truck.

It been Grand Central Station all morning since.

"I wish we were closer!" Ginny moaned, sending a chill up my spine. "I can barely see anything."

"How about you come over here and see about these meatballs," I grumbled.

Ginny laughed, sighed, and pushed away from the window. The ghost outside continued to stare in at me. I ignored it as I always did. Ginny came and took my place at the stove to scoop portions as I stepped back to remove my apron.

"I don't plan to be at Rhonda's long today," I said. "So, I shouldn't be gone but a few minutes."

Ginny looked at me for a few moments, and simply nodded. She didn't ask any questions for once.

"I'll be back," I added, once I was certain she was going to mind her own business.

A minute later, I was on my way to Rhonda's house with my coat on. I'd left my scarf at the shop since the day had proved not to be as windy or chilly as the one before. Still cold enough for an overcoat, but not nearly as cutting. The ghost floated behind me, haunting me, as I made my way to my typical weekday appointment with Rhonda.

When I got to her house, the ghost waited outside the front gate, as it usually did, and I let myself inside. Up on the porch, I took a deep breath and knocked on Rhonda's door. As always, it took a few moments, but she finally found her way through her cavernous house to the door. Swinging it open, she was all smiles and screams as she tried to usher me inside. However, I didn't step past the threshold this time.

When I didn't move, she frowned at me, confused.

"Rhonda," I said, "I'm sorry."

"For what?" she asked.

She stood in the open doorway, folding her arms around herself against the cold and looked at me with pleading eyes.

I shook my head.

"It's obvious," I said, "that Harlan is never going to show up for you. For me. And after thinking about it, I realize it's wrong to keep taking your money every day and letting you have hope that he will one day allow himself to be summoned."

"Are you—"

"I'm firing you as a client," I said. "I'm sorry. But I can't keep trying to coax Harlan into showing up here. He's gone. Whatever that means. I can't get him to come and talk to us. So, you should keep your money and we should stop wasting our time and hope."

Rhonda didn't cry. She didn't plead with me. She seemed to accept what I said with a great sigh.

"All right," she said, frowning.

Then she allowed a smile to take over her face.

"Well," she said, "I guess we've at least proved that he's moved on or whatever spirits do. That's good, right?"

I shrugged. "I just summon 'em. I don't know what comes after the ghost life."

She nodded. "But…"

"I've never seen evidence of anything bad in the afterlife," I said. "At least, nothing worse than what we have here."

I gestured vaguely around and chuckled.

Rhonda snorted.

"Well," she said, "I suppose that's bad enough."

I laughed. "It can be."

I looked at her a moment longer, gave her a nod, then turned.

"Wait," Rhonda said. "Silas."

"Yeah?" I turned back to her.

"You could still come around," she said, thoughtfully. "Maybe once a month? Do a little séance for me. And a few of my friends? Like old times?"

"I—"

"A few hours?" she quickly added. "I'd pay you what I've been paying you for daily visits all month. It could be a little secret club. The girls and I are desperate for excitement. Something silly we can all do. I can't talk to Harlan, but we could talk to others?"

I stared at her for a moment. Ghosts weren't games. But The Lunch Counter didn't pay for itself. My electricity bill couldn't be paid with charm, not that I had a ton to spare.

"Okay."

Rhonda danced in place with glee.

"We'll keep in contact and set the dates up?" she asked quickly.

I nodded.

"I'll text you my available evenings later tonight," I agreed.

Rhonda squealed, said a few pleasantries, then locked me out of the house like the help once more. I made my way off the porch, down the path, and through the gate again. The ghost fell in behind me as I made my way back to the diner, following me the entire way.

When I was putting my coat on the rack by the door inside the diner a few minutes later, Ginny was handing the daily bag of orders to Sal. I greeted her as I rounded the counter and grabbed my apron to tie it back on. The two were in an animated discussion about whatever might be happening at The Eternity Inn. Fortunately, that kept me from having to say anything. Of course, all good things come to an end, and finally they ran out of things to say about the scene across the way.

I was beginning to clean things up when Sal's attention turned to me.

"Have you seen Gary?" she asked when Ginny disappeared into the back.

"Yes," I said, turning to look at her across the counter.

"He's back," Sal said simply. "With the camp."

I nodded.

"Did you have any information for him?" Sal asked, full of hope.

I considered my answer for a moment.

"I think he'll tell you when he's ready," I responded. "If that's good enough for you."

It took her a moment to answer, but Sal finally indicated that she would respect the request. She watched me a moment longer, as if trying to figure something out, glanced at the diner window, then back to me. She started to say something, but decided against it at the last moment.

Shaking the bag at me, as if waving goodbye, she headed to the diner door. Before she could pull the door inward to let herself out, I stopped her.

"Watch out for Gary," I said. "Keep an eye on him."

Sal's brow furrowed as she considered me.

"He has all of you," I said. "But I think he feels like he's alone a lot. Now. Just keep an eye on him."

Sal's frown didn't disappear, but she nodded before heading out the door.

"Going to the bathroom, Si!" Ginny bellowed from the back of the diner.

"Okay!" I bellowed back. "I'll just be up here, waiting to hand out meals!"

She didn't respond, but I knew Ginny had heard me. The Lunch Counter isn't that big, after all. I sighed and propped myself against the counter with my elbows and turned my head to stare out the front window. I ignored the ghost but watched the people and cars in the distance over at The Eternity Inn.

The Grove Gossip would have all the theories and speculations, mixed in with a version of the truth, the following day. I wouldn't have to wait long before everyone knew what had been found. Then cops would be coming around asking questions. As far as I was concerned, I knew nothing about Marcella Washington's disappearance.

She had been found, after all. The cops knew she had been murdered.

I'd done enough.

CHAPTER 20

That night, I allowed myself a rare luxury for autumn. Rare since the nights are usually too chilly, and a luxury because I don't often take time to myself unless there is absolutely no work to be done. However, I found myself out on my front porch that night, a heavy cardigan was enough to protect me against the slight cold. I was sitting in one of the chairs, my laptop on my knees, going through my emails.

Instead of locking myself up in the atrium to do all my work, I decided that a nice night on the porch to organize my evening's summonings would be pleasant. I'd get all of my thoughts together before making my way out to the atrium to summon the ghosts I'd been requested to contact. Or maybe I'd summon them right there on the front porch. It was as safe as the atrium, after all.

However, as it usually goes when I'm trying to have a pleasant evening, I was interrupted. The sun had just disappeared and nighttime was creeping in when I heard the tires on gravel. I closed the laptop and set it on the table by my chair and looked down the driveway. As expected, Danny's truck came into view, headlights bobbling down the long driveway to the house.

When he finally parked and slid down from his truck, I had my arms crossed over my chest, waiting for him. With his hands in his pockets, and his head down, he approached the porch. He didn't walk onto the porch, but instead stood there, his hands in his pants pockets, looking contrite.

"Well," I said, "what do you want?"

Danny looked up and sighed.

"You fired my mom," he said. "Why?"

"Why do you care?"

He stared at me.

"Your dad wasn't going to show up," I said. "It was for the best."

"But why now?"

I shrugged.

"I don't like being involved with one ghost for long," I said. "My business model is I summon, get the information or message needed, report back, and move on with my life. Your dad doesn't want to show up to talk to her. No point in taking all my time and hers bothering with it any longer."

I looked away.

"Séances?" Danny snorted.

"It was a compromise," I said, still looking away. "I make my money, she can talk to other ghosts, she can show off for her friends, and you can't be pissed off about me trying to give her hope about your dad any longer. Though I'm sure you're pissed that I'm a fraud who still takes money from your mother."

"Yeah?"

I shrugged.

"And I don't care," I said.

Danny said nothing; didn't react. He stared at me.

"Is that it?" I asked. "I've got work."

I nodded at the laptop on the table.

"Are you going to invite me in?"

"Not tonight."

Danny looked down.

"Not tonight?" he asked. "Or never again?"

"Not tonight," I said immediately. "I have work. Some things I need to take care of."

He nodded, looking down at the ground.

"Maybe," I said, thinking about it, "give me a few days. I'm free this weekend mostly. Work, but it doesn't take all that long, actually."

Danny looked up, a hopeful gleam in his eye, and nodded. "Okay."

"Go on, then," I said. "If you stick around, people will drive by and see your truck at the fraud's house."

Danny shook his head and rolled his eyes. But he turned and headed back to his truck. I watched him as he walked away. When he grabbed the handle, he turned to look at me.

"I don't actually think you're a fraud," Danny said softly. "I'm just not a believer."

I stared across the distance between us at him.

"I'm too afraid of having hope," he said with a shrug. "Scares me to think that this is it, you know?"

He gestured vaguely.

"Life's kind of crap, you know?" he said. "Why trick yourself into thinking that there's something better? Why have hope? We're born, we live, we do our best, and we die. I'm afraid to believe anything else. Because hope is sometimes scarier than no hope."

I cleared my throat.

"I never said there was anything better," I said. "Just that there is something else."

Danny watched me for a while.

"No bills for ghosts, though," he said, chuckling bitterly. "That's better."

He shook his head and popped the handle of his door. As it swung open, I coughed. Danny turned to look at me.

"Kenny," I said.

Danny's eyes grew wide.

"Your dad called you Kenny sometimes," I said. "For Kenny Loggins. You thought 'Danny's Song' was about you when you were little. So, Harlan called you Kenny when you were little. Made you laugh."

Danny's face was pale when he looked away.

"Kind of a weird song for a small child to be obsessed with," I mumbled. "But kids are weird. You heard 'House at Pooh Corner' on the Loggins and Messina album—"

"How do you know that?" Danny choked out.

I looked him directly in his eyes.

"As you've said," I replied, "I'm a fraud. Right?"

Danny stared at me for a moment, then began looking around frantically. I stared at him, willing my eyes not to move.

"Is he here now?" Danny asked. "Can you—"

"This weekend?" I stopped him. "We'll...yeah. Text me or something."

Danny started to argue, but he saw the look on my face and stopped. His jaw clenched and flexed, his hand balled at his side, but finally, he nodded, leapt into his truck, and closed the door. I gave him a wave as he started it up and turned his truck around, careful to avoid my car on his way.

I watched as he drove down the drive, out of sight. With a sigh, I sat back in my chair and stuck my hands in the pockets of the cardigan. I wasn't certain that Danny believed me still, but what I'd told him definitely had an effect on him. Either way, he'd stop asking the same old question.

What did my dad used to call me?

I was about to reach for my laptop when the moan stopped me.

"*Yoooooou didn't tellll him my message.*"

Frozen in place, unsure how I wanted to handle things, I chewed at my lip. Finally, I looked up at the ghost that had been following me for months. He'd been sitting in the chair next to me all evening as I worked on my laptop on the porch. Harlan Milner was angry with me. But he was always angry with me. I was getting used to it.

"I didn't," I said.

"*Whyyyyy?*"

I stared at the ghost.

"You came to me months ago," I said. "Shortly after your funeral. Found me first thing. I guess you figured you may as well give the fraud medium a chance, huh? Worst you'd do is waste some of the infinite time you had on your hands."

Harlan glared at me.

"I knew something was up with you from the get," I said. "I knew it. And when your wife called me not even three days after the funeral to summon you, I knew it stronger."

The shimmering of Harlan Milner increased.

"Why'd you kill Marcella Washington?" I asked.

He said nothing.

"I mean, I assume, rich man, owns an abandoned hotel. Poor homeless gal needing food and shelter and any bit of money a rich sleazebag would throw at her. I can put two and two together," I said. "But why kill her?"

"I mean," I shrugged, "who would be all that scandalized that you two were meeting at The Eternity Inn? Girl's gotta eat. You were taking advantage of her situation, but it's not the most scandalous thing that happens in the world today. Not by far. In fact, it might put you in line for governor. So…why kill her? Did she threaten to tell Rhonda? Couldn't bear to think of what she'd do? What she'd take in a divorce?"

Harlan said nothing.

"Strangled that poor girl to death and left her body in the tub in the bathroom of the room where you'd meet, huh?" I asked.

When he didn't respond, I nodded, knowing I was right.

"Knew she'd go right to the cupboard you'd set up to trap a fresh ghost," I said. "Tricks you could've learned anywhere online from any decent medium or spiritualist. Anyone worth their salt. Maybe you overheard me talking about it with your wife at one of the séances or perused my website. Then you could seal it shut and her ghost couldn't wander around, find a medium, and rat you out."

Harlan stayed silent.

"I knew there was something up with you," I said. "And it's been confirmed now. So weird that you only sealed up one of your abandoned properties and not the others. Of course, dying shortly after you killed her might've stopped you before you could order the rest shuttered, so I didn't think it *too* weird at the time. At least, not weird enough to be my business. But now I know. It wasn't weird. It was simply the only building you didn't want the folks from the homeless camp to go snooping around in looking for shelter."

Harlan stared into my soul.

"But Gary knew what you did," I said. "He'd followed you that night. Because Marcella was his friend and he was concerned. He knew he wouldn't be believed if he went to the cops. So, he pulled that old cupboard out of the inn, dragged it downstairs, through the cellar, up those stairs, and across to Max's place with a note. At least he knew enough not to open it and let her roam free in her current state."

Harland glowered at me, shimmering in the moonlight that was now pouring down.

"You killed Marcella," I said. "To hell with your message."

"*Danny neeeeeds to knooooooow his mother killed me.*" Harlan pleaded.

I snorted.

"I don't care why Rhonda killed you," I said. "Maybe she figured this all out somehow, too. I don't know. Possibly, she knew about your dalliances with other women. Maybe she just hated your guts after so many years of putting up with you. But when you came to me and told me she killed you, and then she scheduled an appointment with me, I figured enough out to know that she wanted to make sure you were actually gone. She wanted to know if I could talk to you and find out she murdered you. She was checking to see if she was safe. If the cops thought it was a natural death and I couldn't contact you, she was free. She didn't actually care if you were okay in the afterlife."

"*Tellllll him.*"

"As long as your wife isn't a danger to me," I said, "I will never tell him. And I'm pretty sure she believes that I can't contact you for whatever reason. This is done, Harlan. Stop following me. Eye for an eye and all that."

I grabbed my laptop from the table and stood from my chair, staring down at the ghost in the chair next to mine.

"There's no Heaven or Hell that I know of, Harlan," I said. "This is it for you. Wandering around aimlessly, talking to other ghosts, seeing the people you love most age and rot and die and rot some more. A ghost doesn't need God to get their punishment. You can spend all of your time knowing what you did. Knowing what your wife did. Knowing there's absolutely nothing you can do about it. One day, Rhonda will die, and she will have never suffered any in life for what she did to you. And when your wife is dead, this will be over. You two can antagonize each other in death as you did in life. That can be her punishment. And Danny not knowing his two parents are murderous jerks is my gift to him."

TELLLLLL HIM!

Harlan was suddenly out of the chair, looming over me, his teeth bare, ghostly spittle flying and hitting nothing, black ooze seeping from his eyes and nose.

"Careful, Harlan," I said. "Or you'll find yourself in a box. And I can hide a box better than you can hide a body."

It took a second, but Harlan finally returned to his usual form, stared at me a moment, then floated over to the chair and sat. Ghosts sitting. As if they get tired. I snorted.

"Enjoy eternity," I said.

Then I went to the door, into the house, and locked Harlan away. Hopefully for good.

About the Author

Chase Connor spends his days writing about the people who live (loudly and rent-free) in his head when he's not busy being enthusiastic about naps and snacks. Chase started his writing career as a confused gay teen looking for an escape from reality. Ten years later, one of the books he wrote during those years, *Just A Dumb Surfer Dude: A Gay Coming-of-Age Tale*, was published independently. Chase has numerous projects in various stages of completion lined up for publishing. Chase is a multi-genre author, but always with a healthy dollop of gay.

Chase can be reached at
chaseconnor@chaseconnor.com
On Bluesky as chaseconnorbooks
On Instagram as chaseconnorbooks
On Threads as chaseconnorbooks
He can also be found on his website
https://www.chaseconnor.com.
or on Goodreads

SIGN UP FOR THE CHASE CONNOR BOOKS NEWSLETTER AT CHASECONNOR.COM

Chase has several novellas/novels for sale in e-book, paperback, hardback, and audiobook formats wherever books are sold.